Opposing Forces

Opposing Forces

Aldivan Teixeira Torres

GYAN

Published, 2020
Published by
Gyan Publishing House
5, Ansari Road
Daryaganj, New Delhi-110002
Phone: 011-47034999, 9811692060
www.gyanbooks.com
E-mail: books@gyanbooks.com

Printed at: G. Print Process, Delhi.

Cataloging in Publication Data—DK
Courtesy: D.K. Agencies (P) Ltd. <docinfo@dkagencies.com>

Torres, Aldivan Teixeira, author.
Opposing forces / Aldivan Teixeira Torres.
pages cm
Novel.
ISBN 9788121219860

1. Brazilian fiction (English) I. Title.

LCC PR9306.9.T67O67 2019 | DDC 823.92 23

“Dedication”

“First of all, to God, the creator for which everything lives; to the teachers of life that always guided me; to my relatives, although they did not encourage me; to all those who have not yet been able to reunite the “opposing forces” in their lives.”

“The Kingdom of Heaven is like a man who sowed good seed in the field. One night, when all were sleeping, his enemy came and sowed weed among the wheat, and fled. When the wheat grew, and the ears began to form, then also appeared the weed. The employees were looking for the owner, and said unto him. “Sir, didst thou not sow good seed in thy field? Whence came then, the weed?” The owner replied: “‘Was an enemy that has done this.” The employees asked: “Shall we pull out the weed?” The owner replied: “Do not. It could be that upon uprooting the weed, you also get the wheat. Let it grow together until the harvest. And at the time of harvest I will say to the sowers: Start first with the weed and tie it in bundles to be burned. Then gather the wheat into my barn.” Matthew 13:24-30.

Contents

Foreword 11
Acknowledgement 13

1. Introduction 15
2. A New Era 17
3. Preparations 18
4. The Sacred Mountain 20
5. The Hut 25
6. The First Challenge 27
7. The Second Challenge 29
8. The Ghost of the Mountain 31
9. D-Day 34
10. The Young Girl 37
11. The Tremor 43
12. One Day Before the Last Challenge 45
13. The Third Challenge 47
14. The Cave of Despair 49
15. The Miracle 56
16. Exiting the Cave 58
17. The Reunion with the Guardian 62
18. Saying Goodbye to the Mountain 64
19. A Journey Back in Time 66
20. Where am I? 68

21. First Impressions 69
22. The Hotel 71
23. The Dinner 74
24. A Stroll Through the Village 77
25. The Black Castle 81
26. The Chapel Ruins 84
27. The Order 85
28. Meeting of Residents 87
29. Decisive Conversation 89
30. Vision 91
31. The Beginning 93
32. The Railroad 94
33. The Move 95
34. The Arrival at the Bungalow 97
35. Meeting with the Mayor 98
36. Meeting of Farmers 103
37. Back Home 105
38. The Announcement 107
39. The First Day of Work 109
40. The Picnic 114
41. The Descent from the Mountain 124
42. The Major's Abuses 127
43. Mass 130
44. Reflections 133
45. Sucavão 134
46. The Market 137
47. The Case of the Cow 139
48. The Press 141

49. Message 142
50. Meeting 143
51. Confession 146
52. Gossip 147
53. Voyage to Recife 149
54. Return to the Inland 155
55. Arranged Marriage 157
56. Visit 160
57. The Beating 164
58. Gerusa's Cousin 167
59. The "Blessing" 170
60. Phenomena 173
61. A New Friend 174
62. The Day Before the Wedding 176
63. Tragedy 177
64. The Black Cloud 180
65. The Martyrs 181
66. End of the Vision 182
67. Testimony 184
68. Back to the Hotel 186
69. The Idea 188
70. The Figure of the Major 191
71. The Job 194
72. The First Encounter with Christine 195
73. Return to the Castle 198
74. The Message II 200
75. Trip to Climério 201
76. Decision 205

77. The Experience in the Desert 207
78. The Worshipers of Darkness 212
79. The Experience of Possession 213
80. The Prison 215
81. Dialog 216
82. Renato's Visit 218
83. The Third Encounter with Christine 220
84. The Angel's Invocation 223
85. The Final Battle 225
86. The Collapse of the Existing Structures 228
87. Conversation with the Major 229
88. Farewell 231
89. The Return 234
90. At Home 237
91. Epilogue 238

Foreword

Well written, steady paced, smooth flowing read with twists and turns and unpredictable surprises that kept my attention on the pages. If your looking for an easy read with excitement, you've got it. Thanks for sharing this read with us.

Acknowledgement

Firstly, to God. I also thank my family, readers, dreamers and all those who have not yet gathered their opposing forces.

Introduction

"Opposing Forces" presents itself as an alternative to overcoming the great duality that exists in each one of us. How many times in life are we faced with situations in which both alternatives have favorable and unfavorable circumstances and the act of choosing one of them becomes true martyrdom. We must learn to reflect and think carefully about which the true path to be followed is and also the consequences of that choice. Finally, we need to assemble the "opposing forces" of our lives and make them bear fruit. Thus, we can achieve a much desired happiness.

As for the aspect of the book, we can say that it came from a cry that I heard in the cave of despair. This cry was the cause of all the adventures told in the book. Mission accomplished, I hope I have reached my ultimate goal which is to make just one person dream. This is what I propose even more now since we live in a world full of violence, cruelty and injustice. The "opposing forces" never again will be the same after its publication and I cannot wait to start a new adventure together with readers who also intend to do so.

A New Era

After a failed attempt to publish a book, I feel my strength restoring and strengthening. After all, I believe in my talent and I have faith that I am going to fulfill my dreams. I learned that everything happens in its own time and I believe myself to be mature enough to realize my goals. Remember always: When we really want something the world conspires to make it happen. That is how I feel: renewed with strength. Glancing back, I think of the works that I read so long ago which certainly enriched my culture and my knowledge. Books bring us through atmospheres and universes unknown to us. I feel that I need to be part of this history, the great history that is literature. It does not matter if I remain anonymous or become a great author who is recognized worldwide. What is important is the contribution that each one gives to this great universe.

I am happy for this new attitude and I prepare to make a great voyage. This journey will change my fate and also the fates of those who can patiently read this book. Let us go together in this adventure.

Preparations

I pack my suitcase with my personal objects of utmost importance: Some clothes, some good books, my inseparable crucifix and bible and some paper to write. I feel that I will gain a lot of inspiration from this trip. Who knows, maybe I will become the author of an unforgettable story that goes down in history. Before I go, however, I have to bid farewell to all (especially my mother). She is overprotective and will not let me go without a good reason or at least with a promise that I will come back soon. I feel that I will have to, one day, give a cry of freedom and fly as a bird that has created its own wings...and she will have to understand this, because I do not belong to her, but rather to the universe that welcomed me without requiring anything of me in return. It's for the universe that I've decided to become a writer and fulfill my role and develop my talent. When I arrive at the end of the road and have made something of myself I will be ready to enter into communion with the creator and learn a new plan. I'm sure that I will also have a special role in it.

I grab hold of my suitcase and with this I feel anguish rise within me. Questions come to mind and disturb me: What will this trip be like? Will the unknown be dangerous? What precautions should I take? What I do know is that it will be thought provoking for my career and I am willing to do it. I grip my suitcase (again) and before leaving, I seek out my family to say goodbye. My mother is in the kitchen preparing lunch with my sister. I get close and address the crucial issue.

— See this bag? It will be my only companion (except you, readers) in a trip that I am prepared to make. I seek wisdom, knowledge and the pleasure of my profession. I hope that you both understand and approve of the decision I have taken. Come; give me a hug and good wishes.

— My son, forget your goals because they are impossible for poor people like us. I've said a thousand times: You will not be an idol or anything similar. Understand: You were not born to be a great man—Said Julieta, my Mother.

— Listen to our mother. She knows what she's talking about and is absolutely right. Your dream is impossible because you don't have talent. Accept that your mission is just to be a simple math teacher. You will not go any farther than that—Speaked Dalva, my Sister.

— So then, no hugs? Why don't you guys believe that I can be successful? I guarantee you: Even if I pay to realize my dream I will be successful because a great man is he who believes in himself. I will make this journey and I will discover everything there is to reveal. I will be happy because happiness consists of following the path that God enlightens all around us so that we become winners.

Having said that, I direct myself towards the door with the certainty that I will be a winner on this trip: the journey that will take me to unknown destinations.

The Sacred Mountain

A long time ago, I heard of an extremely inhospitable mountain in the area of Pesqueira. It is part of the mountain range of Ororubá (indigenous name) where the indigenous Xukuru people dwell. They say that it became sacred after the death of a mysterious medicine man from one of the Xukuru tribes. It is able to make any wish a reality, as long as the intention is pure and sincere. This is the starting point of my journey whose objective is to make the impossible possible. Do you believe readers? Then remain with me paying special attention to the narrative.

Following the BR-232 highway, reaching the municipality of Pesqueira, approximately fifteen miles from the center, is Mimoso, one of its districts. A modern bridge, recently built, gives access to the place that is between the mountains of Mimoso and Ororubá, bathed by the Mimoso River that runs to the bottom of the valley. The sacred mountain is exactly at this point and that is where I am driving.

The sacred mountain is located next to the district and in a short time I am at the foot of it. My mind wanders through space and distant time imagining unknown situations and phenomena. What awaits me upon climbing this mountain? These certainly will be reviving and stimulating experiences. The mountain is of short stature (2300 ft.) and with each step I feel more confident, but also expectant. Memories come to mind of intense experiences that I have lived during my twenty-six years. In this brief period, there were many fantastic occurrences that made me believe that I was special. Gradually, I can share these memories with you, readers, without guilt. However, this is not the time. I will continue up the path of the mountain in search of all my desires. This is what I hope and for the first time I am tired. I have traveled half of the route. I do not feel physical exhaustion but mainly mental due to strange voices asking me to go back. They insist quite a bit. However, I do not give up easily. I want to reach the top of the mountain for everything it is worth. The mountain breathes for me with airs of change that exude for those who believe in its sanctity. When I get there, I think I will know exactly what to do to reach the path that will lead me through this journey that I have waited for so long. I keep my faith and my goals because I have a God who is the God of the impossible. Let's continue to walk.

I've already gone three quarters of the path but still I'm being chased by the voices. Who am I? Where I'm going? Why do I feel that my life will change dramatically after the experience on the mountain? Apart from the voices, it seems that I'm alone on the road. Could it be that other writers have felt the same thing going down sacred paths? I think that my mysticism will be unlike any other. I have to continue. I have to overcome and withstand all the obstacles. The thorns that injure my body are extremely hazardous to human beings. If I survive this ascent, I would already consider myself a winner.

Step by step, I am closer to the top. I am already just a few feet away from it. The sweat that runs down my body seems to be embedded with sacred scents of the mountain. I stop for a little bit. Will my loved ones be concerned? Well, it really doesn't matter now. I have to think about myself, at the moment, in order to get to the top of the mountain. My future depends on it. Just a few steps more and I arrive at the top. A cold wind blows, tormented voices confuse my reasoning and I do not feel well. The voices shout:

— He succeeded, he shall be awarded! -Is he even worthy? -How did he manage to climb the entire mountain? I am confused and dizzy; I don't think I am well.

Birds cry, and rays of sun caress my face in its entirety. Where am I? I feel as if I had gotten drunk the day before. I try to get up but an arm prevents me. I see that at my side is a middle-aged woman, with red hair and tanned skin.

— Who are you? What happened to me? My whole body hurts. My mind feels confused and vague. Is being at the top of the mountain causing of all this? I think that I should have stayed in my house. My dreams have spurred me up to this point. I climbed the mountain slowly, full of hope for a better future and some direction towards personal growth. However, I practically cannot move. Explain all of this to me, I beg you.

— I am the guardian of the mountain. I am the spirit of the Earth that blows hither and yon. I was sent here because you won the challenge. Do you want to make your dreams come true? I will help you to do so, child of God! You still have many challenges to face. I will prepare you. Do not be afraid. Your God is with you. Rest a little. I'll be back with food and water to meet your needs. In the meantime, relax and meditate as you always do.

Having said that, the lady disappeared from my vision. This disturbing image left me more distressed and full of doubts. What challenges would I have to win? What steps did these challenges consist of? The top of the mountain was really a very splendid and calm place. From up high, one could see the small agglomeration of houses in Mimoso. It is a plateau filled with steep paths full of vegetation on all sides. This sacred place, untouched by nature, would it really accomplish my plans? Would it make me a writer upon my departure? Only time could answer these questions. Since the woman was taking a while, I began to meditate at the top of the mountain. I used the following technique: First, I clear my mind (free of any thoughts). I begin to come into harmony with nature around me, mentally contemplating the entire place. From there, I start to understand that I am part of nature and that we are fully interconnected in a great ritual of communion. My silence is the silence of Mother Nature; my cry is also her cry; Gradually, I begin to feel her desires and aspirations, and vice versa. I feel her distressed cry for help pleading for her life to be saved from human destruction: Deforestation, excessive mining, hunting and fishing, the emission of pollutant gases into the atmosphere and other human atrocities. Likewise, she listens to me and supports me in all my plans. We are completely interlocked during my meditation. All the harmony and complicity has left me totally quiet and concentrated on my desires. Until something changed: I felt the same touch that once awakened me. I opened my eyes, slowly, and saw that I was face to face with the same woman that called herself the guardian of the sacred mountain.

— I see that you understand the secret of meditation. The mountain has helped you to discover a little of your potential. You will grow in many ways. I will help you during this process. First, I ask that you turn to nature to find rafters, slats, props and lines to erect a hut, then firewood to make a bonfire. Night is already approaching and you need to protect yourself against the ferocious beasts. Beginning tomorrow, I will teach you the wisdom of the forest so that you can overcome the real challenge: The cave of despair. Only the pure of heart survive the fire of its analysis. Do you want to make your dreams come true? Then pay the price for them. The universe doesn't give anything for free to anyone. It is us who have to become worthy in order to achieve success. This is a lesson that you must learn, my son.

— I understand. I will hopefully learn everything. I need to overcome the challenge of the cave. I have no idea what it is but I am confident. If I overcame the mountain, I will also succeed in the cave. When I leave, I think that I will be prepared to win and to have success.

— Wait, do not be so confident. You don't know the cave of which I am talking about. Know that many warriors have already been tried by its fire and were destroyed. The cave shows no pity to anyone, not even the dreamers. Have patience and learn everything that I will teach you. Thus, you will become a real winner. Remember: Self-confidence helps, but only with the right amount.

— I understand. Thank you for all your advice. I promise you that I will follow it until the end. When the despair of doubt flogs me I will remind myself of your words and also remind myself that my God will always save me. When there is no

> escape in the dark night of the soul. I will not be afraid. I will beat the cave of despair, the cave which no one has ever escaped!

The woman said goodbye amicably promising return on another day.

The Hut

A new day appears. Birds whistle and sing their melodies, the wind is northeast and its breeze refreshes the sun that rises fiercely hot this time of the year. Currently, it is December and for me this month represents one of the most beautiful months as it is the beginning of school vacation. It is a well-deserved break after a long year dedicated to studies in a college course of Mathematics; The moment you can forget all the integrals, derivatives and polar coordinates. Now I need to worry about all of the challenges that life will throw at me. My dreams depend on it. My back hurts as a result of a bad night of sleep lying on the beaten earth that I prepared as a bed. The hut that I built with incredible effort and the fire that I lit gave me a certain amount of security at night. However, I did hear howling and footsteps outside it. Where have my dreams led me? The answer is to the end of the world where civilization has not yet arrived. What would you do, reader? Would you also risk a trip to make your deepest dreams come true? Let's continue the narrative.

Wrapped in my own thoughts and questions, little did I realize that, at my side, was the strange lady who promised to help me on my way.

— Did you sleep well?

— If well means that I am still whole, yes.

— Before anything, I must warn you that the ground you tread is sacred. Therefore, don't be misled by appearance or by impulsiveness. Today is your first challenge. I will not bring you any more food or water. You will find them by your own account. Follow your heart in all situations. You must prove that you are worthy.

— There is food and water in this underbrush and I should gather it? Look, Madam, I am accustomed to shopping in a supermarket. See this cabin? It has cost me sweat and tears and still I do not think that it is secure. Why don't you grant me the gift that I need? I think I have proved myself to be worthy the moment I climbed that steep mountain.

— Look for food and water. The mountain is only a step in the process of your spiritual improvement. You're still not ready. I must remind you that I do not impart gifts. I have no power to do so. I am only the arrow that indicates the path. The cave is the one who grants your wishes. It is called the cave of despair sought out by those whose dreams have since become impossible.

— I'm going to try. I have nothing else to lose. The cave is my last hope of success.

Having said this, I get up and begin the first challenge. The woman disappeared like smoke.

The First Challenge

At first glance, I see that in front of me is a beaten path. I begin to walk down it. In lieu of the underbrush full of thorns the best would be to follow the trail. The stones that my steps sweep away seem to be telling me something. Can it be that I am on the right path? I think about everything that I left behind in search of my dream: Home, food, clean clothing and my math books. Is this really worth it? I think I will find out. (Time will tell). The strange woman seems not to have told me everything. The more that I walked, the less I found. The top did not seem to be as extensive now that I had arrived. A light...I see a light ahead. I need to go there. I arrive at a spacious clearing where the sun's rays reflect clearly the appearance of the mountain. The trail comes to an end and is reborn into two distinct paths. What do I do? I've been walking for hours and my strength seems to have been exhausted. I sit down a moment to rest. Two paths and two choices. How many times in life are we faced with situations such as this; The entrepreneur who has to choose between the survival of the company or the termination of some employees. The poor mother of the hinterlands in the Northeastern part of Brazil, who has to choose which one of her children to feed; The unfaithful husband who must choose between his wife and his mistress; Anyway, there are many different situations in life. My advantage is that my choice will only affect myself. I need to follow my intuition as the woman recommended.

I get up and I choose the path on the right. I make great strides on this path and it doesn't take me long to glimpse yet another clearing. This time, I encounter a pool of water and some animals around it. They cool themselves in the clear and transparent water. How should I proceed? I've finally found water but it is full of animals. I consult my heart and it tells me that everyone has the right to water. I couldn't just shoo them and deprive them of it as well. Nature gives an abundance of resources for the survival of its people. I am but one of the strands in the web that it weaves. I am not superior to the point that I consider myself the master of it. With my hands, I reach into the water and pour it in a small pot that I brought from home. The first part of the challenge is met. Now I must find food.

I keep walking, on the trail, hoping to find something to eat. My stomach growls as it's already passed noon. I start to look to the sides of the trail. Perhaps the food is inside the forest. How often do we seek the easiest path but it is not the one that leads to success? (Not every climber that follows a trail is the first to reach the top of the mountain). Shortcuts quickly lead you to your target. With this thought, I leave the trail and shortly after find a banana and a coconut tree. It is from them that I will get my food. I have to climb them with the same strength and faith of which I climbed the mountain. I try one, two, three times. I succeed. I will go back to the hut now because I have completed the first challenge.

The Second Challenge

Arriving at my hut, I find the guardian of the mountain who appears more brilliant than ever. Her eyes never stray from my own. I think that I am very special to God. I feel his presence at all times. He resurrects me in every way. When I was unemployed, He opened a door; when I didn't have any opportunities to grow professionally, He gave me new paths; when in times of crisis, He freed me from the bonds of Satan. Anyway, that look of approval from the strange woman reminded me of the man I was up until recently. My current goal was to win regardless of the obstacles that I had to overcome.

— So you won the first challenge. I congratulate you. (Exclaimed the woman). The first challenge aimed to explore your wisdom and your ability to make decisions and share. The two paths represent the "opposing forces" that rule the universe (good and evil). A human being is totally free to choose either path. If one chooses the path on the right one will be illuminated with the help of angels in all moments of his life. That was the path that you chose. However, it is not an easy path. Often, doubts will assault you and you will wonder if this path was even worth it. The people of the world will always be hurtful and take advantage of your good will. Moreover, the confidence you put in others will almost always disappoint you. When you get upset, remember: Your God is strong and he will never abandon you. Never let riches or lust pervert your heart. You are special and because of your value God considers you his son. Never fall from this grace. The path on the left belongs to everyone who rebelled at the Lord's call. All of us are born with a divine mission. However, some deviate from it with materialism, bad influences, corruption of the heart. Those who choose the path on the left do not end up with a pleasant future, Jesus taught us. Every tree that does not give good fruit will be uprooted and thrown into the outer darkness. This is the destiny of bad people because the Lord is fair. That time that you found the water hole and those pitiful animals, your heart spoke louder. Listen to it always and you will go far. The gift of sharing shone on you at that moment and your spiritual growth was surprising. The wisdom that you have helped you to find food. The easiest path is not always the right one to follow. I think that now you are ready for the second challenge. In three days, you will come out of your hut and seek a fact. Act according to your conscience. If you pass, you will move on to the third and final challenge.

— Thank you for accompanying me all this time. I don't know what awaits me in the cave nor do I know what will happen to me. Your contribution is very important to me. Since I climbed the mountain, I feel that my life has changed. I am more calm and confident of what I want. I'll complete the second challenge.

— Very well. I will see you three days from now.

Having said that, the lady disappeared once more. She left me alone in the quietness of the evening along with crickets, mosquitoes and other insects.

The Ghost of the Mountain

Night falls over the mountain. I light a fire and its crackle soothes my heart. It's been two days since I climbed the mountain and it still seems like such a stranger to me. My thoughts wander and land in my childhood: The jokes, the fears, the tragedies. I remember well the day I dressed up as an Indian: With bow, arrow and tomahawk. Now, I was on a mountain that was sacred, precisely because of the death of a mysterious indigenous man (the Medicine Man of the tribe). I have to think of something else for the fear is freezing my soul. Deafening noises surround my hut and I have no idea what or who they are. How does one overcome his fear on an occasion like this? Answer me reader because I don't know. The mountain is still unknown to me.

The noise is moving ever closer and I have nowhere to flee. Leaving the hut would be foolish because I could be swallowed up by ferocious beasts. I'll have to face whatever it is. The noise ceases and a light appears. It makes me even more scared. With a rush of courage, I exclaim:

— In the name of God, who is there?

A voice, nasalized with an obscure twang, responds:

— I am the brave warrior who the cave of despair has destroyed. Give up on your dream or you will have the same fate. I was a small, indigenous man from a village within the Xukuru Nation. I aspired to be the head chief of my tribe and to be stronger than the lion. So I looked to the sacred mountain to accomplish my goals. I won the three challenges that the guardian of the mountain forced upon me. However, upon entering the cave, I was swallowed up by its fire which shattered my heart and my goals. Today, my spirit suffers and is stuck hopelessly to this mountain. Listen to me or you will have the same fate.

My voice froze in my throat and for a moment I could not respond to the tormented spirit. He had left behind shelter, food, a warm family environment. I had two challenges left in the cave, the cave that could make the impossible come true. I would not give up easily on my dream.

— Listen to me, brave warrior. The cave does not perform petty miracles. If I am here, it is for a noble reason. I do not envisage material goods. My dream goes beyond that. I would like to develop myself professionally and spiritually. In short, I want to work doing what I enjoy, earn money responsibly and contribute with my talent for a better universe. I'm not giving up on my dream that easily.

The ghost replied:

— You know the cave and its traps? You are nothing but a poor young man who is unaware of the extreme danger within the path he is following. The guardian is a charlatan who is deceiving you. She wants to ruin you.

The insistence of the ghost annoyed me. Did he know me, by chance? God, in his mercy, would not allow my failure. God and the Virgin Mary were always effectively by my side. The evidence of this was the various apparitions of the Virgin throughout my life. In "Vision of a Medium" (a book that I have not yet published) a scene is described where I am sitting on a bench in a plaza, birds and the wind agitating me, and I am in deep thought about the world and life in general. Suddenly, appeared the figure of a woman that upon seeing me inquired:

— Do you believe in God, my son?

I promptly replied:

— Certainly and with all of my being.

Instantly, she put her hand on my head and prayed:

— May the God of glory cover you in light and grant you many gifts.

Saying this, she went away, and when I realized it, she was no longer by my side. She simply disappeared.

It was the first apparition of the Virgin in my life. Again, disguising herself as a beggar, she came up to me asking for some change. She said she was a farmer and was not yet retired. Readily, I gave her some coins that I had in my pocket. Upon receiving the money, she thanked me and when I realized it, she had disappeared. On the mountain, at that moment, I had not the slightest doubt that God loved me and that he was at my side. Therefore, I responded to the ghost with a certain rudeness.

— I will not listen to your advice. I know my limits and my faith. Go away! Go haunt a house or something. Leave me alone!

The lights went out and I heard the noise of steps leaving the hut. I was free of the ghost.

D-Day

The three days had passed since the second challenge. It was a Friday morning, clear, sunny and bright. I was contemplating the horizon on this morning when the strange woman approached.

— Are you ready? Look for an unusual event in the forest and act according to your principles. This is your second test.

— All right, for three days I've been waiting for this moment. I think that I am prepared.

Hurriedly, I head to the nearest trail that gives access to the forest. My steps followed in an almost musical cadence. What actually was this second challenge? Anxiety took hold of me and my steps accelerated in search of an unknown objective. Right in front emerged a clearing in the trail where it diverged and separated. But when I got there, to my surprise, the bifurcation was gone and I was instead viewing the following scene: a boy, being dragged by an adult, weeping out loud. Emotion took control of me in the presence of injustice and therefore I exclaimed:

— Let the boy go! He is smaller than you and cannot defend himself.

— I will not! I am treating him this way because he does not want to work.

— You monster! Little boys should not have to work. They should study and be well educated. Release him!

— Who will make me, you?

I am completely against violence but at this moment my heart asked me to react before this piece of garbage. The child should be released.

Gently, I pushed the boy away from the brute and then began to beat the man. The bastard reacted and dealt me a few blows. One of them hit me point blank. The world spun and a strong, penetrating wind invaded my entire being: White and blue clouds along with swift birds invaded my mind. In a moment, it seemed like my whole body was floating through the sky. A faint voice called me from afar. In another moment it was as if I going through doors, one after the other as obstacles. The doors were well locked and it took a considerable amount of effort to open them. Each door gave access to either lounges or sanctuaries, alternately. In the first lounge I found young people dressed in white, gathered around a table, on which, in the center, was an open bible. These were the virgins chosen to reign in the future world. A force pushed me out of the room and when I opened the second door I ended up at the first sanctuary. At the edge of the altar, incense sticks with the requests of Brazil's poor were being burned. On the right-hand side, a priest prayed aloud and suddenly began to repeat: Seer! Seer! Seer! Beside him were two women with white shirts. On them was written: Possible dream. Everything began to darken, and when I got my bearings I was dragged violently out and with such speed that it left me a little dizzy. I opened the third door and this time found a meeting of people: A pastor, a priest, a Buddhist, a Muslim, a Spiritualist, a Jew and a representative of African religions. They were arranged in a circle and at the center was a fire and its flames outlined the name, "Union of peoples and paths to God." In the end, they embraced and called me to the group. The fire moved from the center, landed on my hand and drew the word "apprenticeship." The fire was pure light and did not burn. The group broke up, the fire went out and again I was pushed out of the room where I opened the fourth door. The second sanctuary was completely empty and I approached the altar. I knelt in reverence for the Blessed Sacrament, picked up a paper that was on the floor and I wrote my request. I folded the paper and put it at the feet of the image. The voice that was far away gradually became more clear and sharp. I left the sanctuary, opened the door and finally woke up. At my side was the guardian of the mountain.

— So, you are awake. Congratulations! You won the challenge. The second challenge aimed to explore your capacity of self and action. The two paths that represented the "Opposing Forces" have become one and this means that you must travel the right side without forgetting the knowledge that you will have upon meeting the left. Your attitude saved the child despite the fact that he didn't need it. That whole scene was my own mental projection to evaluate you. You took the right approach. The majority of people when faced with scenes of injustice prefer not to interfere. Omission is a serious sin and the person becomes an accomplice of the offender. You gave of yourself, as Jesus Christ did for us. This is a lesson that you will take with you your whole life.

— Thank you for congratulating me. I would always act in favor of those who have been excluded. What puzzles me is the spiritual experience I had earlier. What does it mean? Could you explain to me, please?

— We all have the ability to penetrate other worlds through thought. This is what is called astral travel. There are some experts in relation to this matter. What you saw must be related to your or another person's future, you never know.

— I understand. I climbed the mountain, completed the first two challenges and I must be growing spiritually. I think that soon I will be ready to face the cave of despair. The cave that performs miracles and makes dreams more profound.

— You must perform the third and I will tell you what it is tomorrow. Wait for instructions.

— Yes, General. I'll be waiting anxiously. This Child of God, as you called me, is very hungry and will prepare a soup for later. You are invited, ma'am.

— Wonderful. I love soup. I will use this to my advantage to get to know you better.

The strange lady departed and left me alone with my thoughts. I went looking in the forest for the ingredients for the soup.

The Young Girl

The mountain had already turned dark when the soup was ready. The cold wind of the night and the cri-cri-cri of insects makes the environment evermore rural. The strange lady has not yet come to the hut. I hope to have everything in order by the time she arrives. I taste the soup: It really was good although I did not have all the necessary condiments. I step outside of the hut for a little bit and contemplate the heavens: The stars are witnesses of my efforts. I went up the mountain, found its guardian, completed two challenges (one more difficult than the other), met a ghost and I am still standing. "The poor strive more for their dreams." I look at the arrangement of the stars and their luminosity. Each has its own importance in the great universe that we live in. People are also important in the same way. They are white, black, rich, poor, of religion A, or religion B or of any belief system. They are all children with the same father. I also want to take my place in this universe. I am a thinking being without limits. I think that a dream is priceless but I am willing to pay for it in order to enter the cave of despair. I contemplate the heavens once more and then go back to the hut. I wasn't surprised to find guardian there.

— Have you been here long? I hadn't realized.

— You were so concentrated in contemplating the heavens that I did not want to break the spell of the moment. In addition to that, I feel at home.

— Very good. Sit on this improvised bench that I made. I will serve the soup.

With the soup still hot, I served the strange lady in a gourd that I found in the forest. The wind whipping in the night caressed my face and whispered words in my ear. Who was that strange lady that I was serving? I wonder if she really wanted to destroy me as the ghost hinted. I had many doubts about her and this was a great opportunity to clear them.

— Is the soup good? I prepared it with great care.

— It's wonderful! What did you use to prepare it?

— It is made of stones. Just kidding! I bought a bird from a hunter and used some natural seasonings from the forest. But, changing the subject, who are you really?

— It shows good hospitality for the host to talk first about himself. It's been four days since you arrived here at the top of the mountain and I am not even sure what your name is.

— Very well. But it is a long story. Get ready. My name is Aldivan Teixeira Tôrres and I teach college level Mathematics. My two great passions are literature and math. I've always been a lover of books and ever since I was very small I have wanted to write one of my own. When I was in my first year of high school I gathered some excerpts from the books of Ecclesiastes, wisdom and proverbs. I was very happy in spite of the texts not being mine. I showed everyone, with great pride. I finished High School, took a computer course and stopped studying for a while. After that I tried a technical course at a local college. However, I realized it wasn't my field by a sign of fate. I was prepared for an internship in this area. However, the day before the test a strange force demanded continuously for me to give up. The more time passed, the more pressure I felt from this force until I decided to not take the test. The pressure subsided and my heart was calmed also. I think it was fate that made me not go. We must respect our own limits. I did a number of tenders, was approved and currently hold the role of administrative assistant of education. Three years ago I received another sign of fate. I had some problems and I ended up having a nervous breakdown. I started then to write and in a short time it helped me to improve. The result was the book "Vision of a Medium" which I have not yet published. All of this showed me that I was able to write and have a dignified profession. This is what I think: I want to work doing what I like and I want to be happy. Is that too much for a poor person to ask?

— Of course not, Aldivan. You have talent and that is rare in this world. At the right time you will succeed. Victorious are those who believe in their dreams.

— I do believe. That's why I'm here in the middle of nowhere where the commodities of civilization have not yet arrived. I found a way to climb the mountain, to overcome the challenges. All that is left now is for me to enter the cave and carry out my dreams.

— I'm here to help you. I have been the guardian of the mountain ever since it became sacred. My mission is to help all dreamers seeking the cave of despair. Some seek to make material dreams come true such as money, power, social ostentation or other selfish dreams. All have failed so far, and they have not been few. The cave is fair with its granting of wishes.

The conversation continued in a lively manner for some time. I was gradually losing interest in it as a strange voice called me out of the hut. Each time that this voice called me I felt compelled to go out of curiosity. I had to go. I wanted to know what that strange voice in my thoughts meant. Gently, I said farewell to the woman and set out in the direction indicated by the voice. What awaits me? Let us continue together, reader.

The night was cold and the insistent voice remained in my mind. There was a kind of strange connection between us. I had already walked a few feet outside of the hut but it seemed to be miles by the fatigue that my body was feeling. The instructions that I mentally received guided me in the darkness. A mixture of tiredness, fear of the unknown and curiosity controlled me. Whose strange voice was this? What did she want with me? The mountain and its secrets... Ever since I got to know the mountain, I have learned to respect it. The guardian and her mysteries, the challenges that I had to confront, the encounter with the ghost; it all became special. It was not the highest in the northeast or even the most impressive, but it was sacred.

The myths of the medicine man and my dreams have led me to it. I want to win all the challenges, enter the cave and make my request. I will be a changed man. I will no longer be just me, but I will be the man who overcame the cave and its fire. I remember well the words of the guardian, not to trust too much. I remember the words of Jesus who said:

— He who believeth in me shall have eternal life.

The risks involved will not make me desist of my dreams. It is with this thought that I am ever more faithful. The voice becomes stronger and stronger. I think that I am arriving at my destination. Right in front, I see a hut. The voice tells me to go there.

The hut and its illuminating bonfire are in a spacious, flat place. A young, tall, thin girl with dark hair is grilling a type of snack on the fire.

— So, you have arrived. I knew that you would answer my call.

— Who are you? What do you want from me?

— I am another dreamer who wants to enter the cave.

— What special powers do you have to call out to me with your mind?

— It's telepathy, silly. Aren't you familiar with it?

— I've heard of it. Could you teach me?

— You will learn one day but not from me. Tell me what dream brings you here?

— Before all, my name is Aldivan. I climbed the mountain in hopes of finding my opposing forces. They shall define my destiny. When someone is able to control their opposing forces they will be able to perform miracles. That's what I need to accomplish my dream of working in an area that I enjoy and with that I will make many souls dream. I want to go into the cave not only for me but for the entire universe that has provided me these gifts. I will have my place in the world and that is how I will be happy.

— My name is Nadja. I am an inhabitant of the Pernambucan coast. In my land I've heard talk of this miraculous mountain and its cave. Immediately I was interested in making the journey here even though I thought that everything was merely a legend. I gathered my stuff, left, arrived in Mimoso and went up the mountain. I hit the jackpot. Now that I'm here I will go into the cave and will fulfill my wish. I will be a great Goddess, adorned with power and riches. All will serve me. Your dream is just silly. Why ask for a little if we can have the world?

— You are mistaken. The cave does not perform petty miracles. You will fail. The guardian will not allow you to enter. To enter the cave you must win three challenges. I have already conquered two of the stages. How many have you won?

— How dumb, challenges and guardians. The cave only respects the strongest and most confident. I will achieve my desires tomorrow and no one will stop me, you hear?

— You know best. When you regret it, it will be too late. Well, I guess I'll be going. I need some rest because it is late. As for you, I cannot wish you good luck in the cave because you want to be greater than God himself. When humans reach this point they destroy themselves.

— Nonsense, you're all words. Nothing will make me go back on my decision.

Seeing that she was adamant I gave up, feeling sorry for her. How can people become so petty sometimes? The human being is only worthy when he fights for righteous and egalitarian ideals. Walking the trail, I remembered the times I've been wronged whether it was by an ill-marked examination or even from the neglect of others. It makes me unhappy. On top of this, my family is totally against my dream and does not believe in me. It hurts. One day they will see reason and see that dreams can be possible. On that day, after all is said and done, I'll sing my victory and I will glorify the Creator. He gave me everything and only required me to share my gifts because, as the Bible says, do not light a lamp and put it under the table. Rather put it on top for all to applaud and be enlightened. The trail breaks and immediately I see the hut that has cost me so much sweat to build. I need to go to sleep because tomorrow is another day and I have plans for me and for the world. Good night, readers. Until the next chapter...

The Tremor

A new day begins. Light appears, the breeze of the morning caress my hair, birds and insects are having a celebration, and the vegetation seems to be reborn. It happens every day. I rub my eyes, wash my face, brush my teeth and take a bath. This is my routine before breakfast. The forest offers neither advantages nor options. I am not accustomed to this. My mother spoiled me to the point of serving me my coffee. I eat my breakfast in silence but something weighs on my mind. What will the third and final challenge be? What will happen to me in the cave? There are so many questions without answers it makes me dizzy. The morning progresses and with it so do my palpitations, fears and chills. Who was I now? Certainly not the same. I went up a sacred mountain looking for a destiny that not even I knew about. I found the guardian and discovered new values and a world larger than I ever imagined existed before. I won two challenges and now only had to face the third. A chilling third challenge that was distant and unknown. The leaves around the hut move ever-so-slightly. I have learned to understand nature and its signals. Someone is approaching.

— Hello! Are you there?

I jumped, changed the direction of my gaze and contemplated the mysterious figure of the guardian. She seems happier and even rosy despite her apparent age.

— I am here, as you can see. What news have you brought for me?

— As you know, today I come to announce your third and final challenge. It will be held on your seventh day here on the mountain because that is the maximum time that a mortal can remain here. It is simple and consists of the following: Kill the first man or beast that you encounter upon leaving your hut on the very same day. Otherwise you will not be entitled to enter into the cave which grants you your deepest desires. What do you say? Isn't that easy?

— How so? Kill? Do I look like an assassin?

— It's the only way for you to enter into the cave. Prepare yourself, because there are only two days and...

An earthquake with a magnitude of 3.7 on the Richter scale shakes the entire top of the mountain. The tremor leaves me dizzy and I think that I am going to faint. More and more thoughts come to mind. I feel my strength depleting and feel handcuffs that forcefully secure my hands and my feet. In a flash, I see myself as a slave, working in fields dominated by masters. I see the shackles, the blood and hear the cries of my companions. I see the richness, pride and treachery of the colonels. I also see the cry of freedom and justice for the oppressed. Oh, how the world is unfair! While some win others are left to rot, forgotten. The handcuffs break. I am partially free. I'm still discriminated against, hated and wronged. I still see the evil of the white men who call me "nigger." I still feel inferior. Again I hear the cries of clamor but now the voice is clear, sharp and known. The tremor disappears and little by little I regain consciousness. Someone lifts me up. Still a little woozy, I exclaim:

— What happened?

The guardian, in tears, can't seem to find an answer.

— My son, the cave has just destroyed another soul. Please win the third challenge and defeat this curse. The universe is conspiring for your victory.

— I do not know how to win. Only the creator's light can illuminate my thoughts and my actions. I guarantee: I'm not going to give up on my dreams easily.

— I trust in you and in the education that you have received. Good luck, Child of God! See you soon!

Having said that, the strange lady departed and was dissolved in a puff of smoke. Now I was alone and needed to prepare for the final challenge.

One Day Before the Last Challenge

It's been six days since I went up the mountain. This entire time of challenges and experiences has made me grow a lot. I can more easily understand nature, myself and others. Nature marches to its own beat and is opposed to the pretensions of human beings. We deforest the forests, pollute the waters, and release gases into the atmosphere. What do we get out of it? What really matters to us, money or our own survival? The consequences are there: Global warming, reduction of flora and fauna, natural disasters. Does man not see that this is all his fault? There is still time. There is time for life. Do your part: Save water and energy, recycle waste, do not pollute the environment. Require your government to commit to environmental issues. It's the least we can do for ourselves and for the world. Coming back to my adventure, once I went up the mountain, I better understood my wishes and my limits. I understood that dreams are only made possible as long as they are noble and righteous. The cave is fair and if I win the third challenge, it will make my dream come true. When I won the first and second challenges I came to better understand the wishes of others. The majority of people dream to have riches, social prestige and high levels of command. They no longer see what is best in life: Professional success, love and happiness. What makes the human being really special are his qualities that shine through his work. Power, wealth, and social ostentation do not make anyone happy. This is what I am looking for in the sacred mountain: Happiness and total domain of the "opposing forces." I need to go out for a little bit. Step by step, my feet lead me outside of the hut that I built. I hope for a sign of destiny.

The sun heats up, the wind gets stronger and no sign appears. How will I win the third challenge? How will I live with the failure if I am not able to carry out my dream? I try to move the negative thoughts out of my mind but the fear is stronger. Who was I before climbing the mountain? A young man, totally insecure, afraid to face the world and its people. A young man who one day fought in court for his rights but they were not granted. The future has shown me that this was best. Sometimes we win by losing. Life has taught me that. Some birds screech around me. They seem to understand my concern. Tomorrow will be a new day, the seventh on top of the mountain. My destiny is in jeopardy with this third challenge. Pray, readers, that I may win.

The Third Challenge

A new day appears. The temperature is pleasant and the sky is blue in all its immensity. Lazily, I get up rubbing my sleepy eyes. The big day has arrived and I am prepared for it. Before anything, I need to prepare my breakfast. With the ingredients that I managed to find the day before, it will not be so scarce. I prepare the pan and start cracking open the appetizing chicken eggs. The fat splashes and almost hits my eye. How many times in life, others seem to hurt us with their anxieties. I eat my breakfast, rest a little and prepare my strategy. The third challenge seems to be anything but easy. Killing for me is unthinkable. Well, even so, I will have to confront it. With this resolution, I start to walk and soon I am out of the hut. The third challenge starts here and I prepare for it. I take the first trail and I start to walk. The trees by the road of the path are wide with deep roots. What really am I looking for? Success, victory and achievement. However, I will not do anything that goes against my principles. My reputation goes before fame, success and power. The third challenge is bothering me. Killing for me is a crime even if it is only an animal. On the other hand, I want to enter into the cave and make my request. This represents two "opposing forces" or "opposite paths."

I remain on the trail and pray that I do not find anything. Who knows, maybe the third challenge would be dismissed. I don't think that the guardian would be that generous. The rules have to be followed by all. I stop a little and cannot believe the scene that I see: an ocelot and its three cubs, frolicking around me. That's it. I will not slay the mother of three cubs. I do not have the heart. Goodbye success, goodbye cave of despair. Enough dreams. I did not complete the third challenge and I am leaving. I will return to my house and to my loved ones. Hurriedly, I go back to the cabin to pack my bags. I do not complete the third challenge.

The cabin is torn down. What is the meaning of all this? A hand touches my shoulder lightly. I look back and I see the guardian.

— My congratulations, dear! You have fulfilled the challenge and now have the right to enter into the cave of despair. You won!

The strong embrace she imparted on me then left me even more confused. What was this woman saying? My dream and the cave could be found after all? I didn't believe it.

— What do you mean? I did not complete the third challenge. Look at my hands: They are clean. I will not stain my name with blood.

— Don't you know? Do you think that a child of God would be capable of such an atrocity as that which I asked? I have no doubt that you are worthy enough to realize your dreams, although it may take a while for them to become reality. The third challenge thoroughly evaluated you and you demonstrated unconditional love for God's creatures. This is the most important thing for a human being. One more thing: Only a pure heart will survive the cave. Keep your heart and your thoughts clean to overcome it.

— Thank you, God! Thank you, life, for this chance. I promise not to disappoint you.

Emotion took a hold of me as it never had before I climbed the mountain. Was the cave really capable of performing miracles? I was about to find out.

The Cave of Despair

After winning the third challenge I was ready to enter the dreaded cave of despair, the cave that realizes impossible dreams. I was yet another dreamer who was going to try their luck. Ever since I went up the mountain I was no longer the same. Now I was confident in myself and in the wonderful universe that held me. The previous embrace that the strange woman gave me also left me more relaxed. Now she was there by my side supporting me in every way. This was the support that I never got from my loved ones. My inseparable suitcase is under my arm. It was time for me to say farewell to that mountain and its mysteries. The challenges, the guardian, the ghost, the young girl and the mountain itself which seemed to be alive, they all have helped me to grow. I was ready to leave and face the dreaded cave. The guardian is by my side and will accompany me on this journey to the cave's entrance. We leave because the sun is already descending towards the horizon. Our plans are in total harmony. The vegetation around the trail that we have traveled and the noise of animals makes the environment very rural. The guardian's silence during the whole course seems to foretell the dangers that the cave encloses. We stop a little. The voices of the mountain seem to want to say something to me. I take this opportunity to break the silence.

— Can I ask something? What are these voices that torment me so much?

— You hear voices. Interesting. The sacred mountain has the magic ability to reunite all dreaming hearts. You are able to feel these magical vibrations and interpret them. However, do not pay much attention to them because they may lead you to failure. Try to concentrate on your own thoughts and their activity will be less. Be careful. The cave is able to detect your weaknesses and use them against you.

— I promise to take care of myself. I do not know what awaits me in the cave but I have faith that the illuminating spirits will help me. My destiny is at stake and to some extent that of the rest of the world too.

— Alright, we've rested enough. Let's continue to walk because it won't be long until sunset. The cave should be about a quarter of a mile from here.

The rumble of footsteps resumes. A quarter of a mile separated my dream from its realization. We are on the west side of the top of the mountain where the winds are ever stronger. The mountain and its mysteries... I think that I will never know it fully. What motivated me to climb it? The promise of the impossible becoming possible and my adventurer and scouting instincts. In reality, what was possible and an everyday routine were killing me. Now I was feeling alive and ready to overcome challenges. The cave is approaching. I can already see its entrance. It seems imposing, but I am not discouraged. A range of thoughts invade my entire being. I need to control my nerves. They could betray me in time. The guardian signals to stop. I obey.

— This is the closest that I can get to the cave. Listen well to what I am going to say because I will not repeat it: Before entering, pray one Our Father for your guardian angel. It will protect you from the dangers. When you enter, proceed with caution in order not to fall into traps. After traveling the cave's main walkway a certain amount of time you will encounter three options: Happiness, failure and fear. Choose happiness. If you choose failure, you will remain a poor madman who used to dream. If you choose fear you will lose yourself completely. Happiness gives access to two more scenarios that are unknown to me. Remember: Only the pure of heart can survive the cave. Be wise and fulfill your dream.

— I understand. The moment I have been waiting for ever since I went up the mountain has arrived. Thank you, guardian, for all your patience and zeal with me. I'll never forget you or the moments we have spent together.

Anguish took hold of my heart as I said goodbye to her. Now it was just me and the cave, a duel that would change the history of the world and also my own. I look right at it and get my flashlight from my suitcase to illuminate the path. I am ready to enter. My legs seem frozen before this giant. I need to gather the strength to continue on the path. I'm Brazilian and I never, ever give up. I take my first steps and I have the slight feeling that someone is accompanying me. I think I am very special to God. He treats me as if I were his son. My steps begin to accelerate and finally I enter the cave. The initial fascination is overwhelming but I need to be cautious because of the traps. The humidity of the air is high and the cold intense. Stalactites and stalagmites fill practically everywhere around me. I've gone about fifty yards in and the chills begin to give me goosebumps all over my body. Everything I've gone through before climbing the mountain begins to come to my mind: The humiliations, the injustices and the envy of others. It seems that every one of my enemies is within that cave waiting for the best time to attack me. With a spectacular jump, I overcome the first trap. The cave's fire almost devoured me. Nadja was not so lucky. Clinging to a stalactite from the ceiling that miraculously endured my weight, I managed to survive. I need to get down and continue my journey towards the unknown. My steps accelerate but with caution. Most people are in a hurry, in a hurry to win, or to complete goals. Fantastic agility has just saved me from a second trap. Countless spears were heaved towards me. One of them came as close as to scratch my face. The cave wants to destroy me. I have to be more careful from now on. It's been approximately one hour since I entered the cave and still I have not come to the point of which the guardian spoke. I should be close. My steps continue, accelerated, and my heart gives a warning sign. Sometimes, we don't pay attention to the signs our body gives. This is when failure and disappointment happen. Fortunately, that is not the case for me. I hear a very loud noise coming in my direction. I start to run. In a few moments, I realize that I am being chased by a giant stone tumbling at a great speed. I run for a while and with a sudden movement I am able to get away from the rock, finding shelter at the side of the cave. When the stone passes, the front part of the cave is closed and then right in front three doors appear. They represent happiness, failure and fear. If I choose failure, I will never be anything but a poor madman who one day dreamed of becoming a writer. People will take pity on me. If I choose fear I will never grow nor be known by the world. I could hit rock bottom and lose myself forever. If I choose happiness I will continue with my dream and I will pass into the second scenario.

There are three options: A door to the right, to the left and one in the middle. Each one of them represents one of the options: Happiness, failure or fear. I have to make the right choice. I have learned with time to overcome my fears: Fear of the dark, fear of being alone and fear of the unknown. Also I am not afraid of success or the future. Fear must represent the door on the right. Failure is the result of poor planning. I've failed a few times but it has not made me give up on my goals. Failure should serve as a lesson for a later victory. Failure must represent the door on the left. Finally, the middle door must represent happiness because the righteous turn neither toward the right nor to the left. Righteousness is always happy. I gather my strength and I choose the door in the middle. Upon opening it I have ample access to a lounge and on the roof is written the name Happiness. In the center is a key that gives access to another door. I really was right. I fulfilled the first step. That leaves me two more. I get the key and try it in the door. It fits perfectly. I open the door. It gives me access to a new gallery. I start to go down it. A multitude of thoughts flood my mind: What will the new traps be that I must face? What kind of scenario will this gallery lead me to? There are many unanswered questions. I continue to walk and my breathing becomes strained because the air is increasingly scarce. I've already gone about a tenth of a mile and I must remain attentive. I hear a noise and fall to the ground to protect myself. It's the noise of small bats that shoot around me. Will they suck my blood? Are they carnivores? Luckily for me, they disappear into the vastness of the gallery. I see a face and my body trembles Is it a ghost? No. It is flesh and blood and it is coming at me, ready to fight. It is one of the priest ninjas of the cave. The fight begins. He is very fast and tries to hit me in a crucial place. I try to escape his attacks. I fight back with some moves I learned watching movies. The strategy works. It frightens him and he moves back a little. He strikes back with his martial arts but I'm prepared for it. I hit him on the head with a rock I picked up in the cave. He falls unconscious. I'm totally averse to violence but in this case it was strictly necessary. I would like to go to the second scenario and discover the secrets of the cave. I begin walking again and I remain attentive and protect myself against any new traps. With the humidity low, a wind blows and I become more comfortable. I feel the currents of positive thoughts sent by the Guardian. The cave darkens even more, transforming itself. A virtual labyrinth shows itself straight ahead. Another of the cave's traps. The entrance of the labyrinth is perfectly visible. But where is the exit? How do I enter and not get lost? I only have one option: Cross the labyrinth and take the risk. I build my courage and start to take the first steps towards the entrance of the maze. Pray, reader, that I find the exit. I have no strategy in mind. I think I should use my knowledge to get me out of this mess. With courage and faith, I delve into the maze. It seems more confusing on the inside than out. Its walls are wide and turn in zigzags. I'm beginning to remember the moments in life where I found myself lost as if in a maze. The death of my father, so young, was a real blow in my life. The time I spent unemployed and not studying also made me feel lost as if in a maze. I now was in the same situation. I keep walking and there seems to be no end to the labyrinth. Have you ever felt desperate? That was how I felt, totally desperate. This is why it has the name the cave of despair. I gather my last bit of strength and get up. I need to find the way out at any cost. One last idea hits me; I look up to the ceiling and see many bats. I will follow one of them. I'll call him "wizard." A wizard would be able to conquer a maze. This is what I need. The bat flies with great speed and I have to keep up with it. It's good that I am physically fit, almost an athlete. I see the light at the end of the tunnel, or better yet, at the end of the labyrinth. I am saved.

The end of the labyrinth has led me to a strange scene in the gallery of the cave. A room made of mirrors. I walk around carefully for fear of breaking something. I see my reflection in the mirror. Who am I now? A poor young dreamer about to discover his destiny. I look particularly worried. What does all this mean? The walls, ceiling, the floor everything is composed of glass. I touch the surface of a mirror. The material is so fragile but faithfully reflects the aspect of the one's self. In an instant distinct images appear in three of the mirrors, a child, a young person holding a coffin, and an old man. They are all me. Is it a vision? Really I do have child-like aspects such as purity, innocence and faith in people. I don't think that I want to get rid of these qualities. The young man of fifteen represents a painful phase in my life: The loss of my father. Despite his rigid and aloof ways, he was my father. I still remember him with nostalgia. The elderly man represents my future. How will it be? Will I be successful? Married, single or even widowed? I do not want to be a revolting or hurt old man. Enough with these images. My present is now. I am a young man of twenty-six, with a degree in Mathematics, a writer. I am no longer a child, nor the fifteen year old who lost his father. I am also not an old man. I have my future ahead of me and I want to be happy. I am not any of these three images. I am myself. With an impact, the three mirrors in which the individuals appeared break and a door appears. It is my entry into the third and last scenario.

I open the door that gives access to a new gallery. What awaits me in the third scenario? Together let us continue, reader. I begin to walk and my heart accelerates as if I was still in the first scene. I have overcome many challenges and pitfalls and already consider myself a winner. In my mind, I seek out the memories of the past when I played in small caves. The situation now is completely different. The cave is huge and full of traps. My flashlight is almost dead. I continue to walk and straight ahead emerges a new trap: Two doors. The "opposing forces" shout within me. It is necessary to make a new choice. One of the challenges comes to mind, and I remember how I had the courage to overcome it. I chose the path on the right. The situation is different though because I am inside of a dark, damp cave. I have made my choice but also begin to remember the words of the guardian who spoke about learning. I need to get to know the two forces in order to have total control over them. I choose the door on the left. I open it slowly; fearful of what it may be hiding. As I open it, I contemplate a vision: I am inside of a shrine, filled with images of saints with a chalice on the altar. Could it be the Holy Grail, the lost chalice of Christ which gives eternal youth to those who drink from it? My legs are shaking. Impulsively, I run toward the chalice and begin to drink from it. The wine tastes heavenly, of the Gods. I feel dizzy, the world spins, the angels sing and the grounds of the cave shudder. I have my first vision: I see a Jew named Jesus, together with his apostles, healing, freeing and teaching new perspectives to his people. I see the entire trajectory of his miracles and his love. I also see the betrayal of Judas and the Devil acting behind his back. Finally, I see his resurrection and glory. I hear a voice saying to me: Make your request. Resounding with joy I exclaim: I want to become the Seer!

The Miracle

Soon after my request, the shrine trembles, fills with smoke and I can hear altered voices. What they reveal is completely secret. A small fire rises from the chalice and lands in my hand. Its light is penetrating and illuminates the entire cave. The walls of the cave transform and give way to a small door that appears. It opens and a strong wind begins to push me to it. All of my efforts come to mind: My dedication to studying, the way I have perfectly followed God's laws, the ascent of the mountain, the challenges, and even this very passage into the cave. All this has brought me an astonishing spiritual growth. I was now prepared to be happy and to fulfill my dreams. The much dreaded cave of despair had forced me to make my request. I do remember also in this sublime moment all of those who have contributed to my victory directly or indirectly: My primary school teacher, Mrs. Socorro, who taught me reading and writing, my teachers of life, my school and work friends, my family and the guardian that helped me to overcome the challenges and this very cave. The strong wind keeps pushing me towards the door and soon I will be inside the secret chamber.

The force that pushed me finally ceases. The door closes. I am in an extremely large chamber that is high and dark. On the right side is a mask, a candle and a Bible. On the left is a cape, a ticket and a crucifix. In the center, up high, is an interesting looking circular apparatus made of iron. I walk toward the right side: I put on the mask, grab the candle and open the Bible to a random page. I walk toward the left side: I put on the cape, write my name and alias on the ticket and secure the crucifix with the other hand. I walk towards the center and I position myself exactly below the apparatus. I utter the four magical letters: S-e-e-r. Immediately, a circle of light is emitted by the device and envelopes me completely. I smell the incense that is burned every day in memory of the great dreamers: Martin Luther King, Nelson Mandela, Mother Teresa, Francis of Assisi and Jesus Christ. My body vibrates and begins to float. My senses begin to be awakened and with them I am able to recognize feelings and intentions more profoundly. My gifts are strengthened and with them I am able to perform miracles in time and space. The circle closes increasingly and every feeling of guilt, intolerance and fear is erased from my mind. I am almost ready: A sequence of visions start to appear and confuse me. Finally the circle goes out. In an instant, a sequence of doors is opened and with my new gifts I can see, feel and hear perfectly. The screams of characters wanting to manifest, distinct times and places begin to appear and significant questions begin to corrode my heart. The challenge of becoming clairvoyant is launched.

Exiting the Cave

With everything accomplished, all that was left now was for me to leave the cave and make my true journey. My dream was granted and now just needed to be put to work. I start to walk and with little time I leave behind the secret chamber. I feel that no other human being will ever have the pleasure to enter it. The cave of despair will never be the same again after I leave victorious, confident and happy. I return to the third scenario: The images of the saints remain intact and seem to be happy with my victory. The cup has fallen over and is dry. The wine was delicious. I work my way calmly around the third scenario and feel the atmosphere of the place. It really is as sacred as the cave and the mountain. I yell for joy and the echo produced extends across the cave. The world will no longer be the same after the Seer. I stop, think and contemplate myself in every way. With a final farewell kiss I leave the third scenario and I return to the same door on the left which I chose. The path of the Seer will not be an easy one because it will be challenging to fully control the opposing forces of the heart and then having to teach that to others. The path on the left, which was my option, represents knowledge and continuous learning whether with hidden forces, repentance or death itself. The walk becomes exhaustive as the cave is extensive, dark and very humid. The challenge of the Seer may be greater than I realize: The challenge of reconciling hearts, lives and feelings. That is not all: I have yet to take care of my own path. The gallery becomes narrow and with it so do my thoughts. My feelings of homesick surge, as well as nostalgia for mathematics and my own personal life. Lastly, comes the nostalgia of myself. I hasten my steps and soon I am in the second scenario. Broken mirrors now represent the parts of my mind that were preserved and expanded: the good feelings, the virtues, the gifts and the capacity to recognize when

I have erred. The scenario of mirrors is a reflection of my own soul. This self-knowledge I will take with me my entire life. Still stored in my memory are the figures of the child, the young fifteen year old and the elderly man. They are three of my many faces which I preserve because they are my own history. I leave the second scenario and with it I leave my memories. I am in the gallery that leads to the first scenario. My expectations of the future and my hope are renewed. I am the Seer, an evolved and special being, destined to make many souls dream. The post-cave period will serve as training and improvement of pre-existing skills. I go a little further and catch a glimpse of the labyrinth. This challenge has almost destroyed me. My salvation was Wizard, the bat that helped me find the exit. Now I do not need him anymore because with my clairvoyant powers I can easily pass by him. I have the gift of guidance in five planes. How often do we feel as if we were lost in a maze: When we lose jobs; When we are disappointed with the great love of our lives; When we defy the authority of our superiors; When we lose hope and the ability to dream; When we stop being apprentices of life and when we lose the ability to direct our own destiny. Remember: The universe predisposes the person but it is we who have to go for it and prove that we are worthy. That is what I did. I went up the mountain, performed three challenges, entered the cave, defeated its traps and I reached my destination. I get through the labyrinth and it doesn't make me that happy since I already won the challenge. I intend to seek new horizons. I've walked about two miles between the secret chamber, the second and the third scenarios and with this realization I feel a little tired. I feel sweat trickling down; I also feel the air pressure and low humidity. I approach the ninja, my great adversary. He still seems knocked out. I'm sorry I treated you that way but my dream, my hope and my destiny was at stake. One has to make important decisions in important situations. Fear, shame, and morality only get in the way instead of helping. I caress his face and I try to restore life in his body. I act in this way because we are no longer adversaries but companions of this episode. He raises and with a deep bow he congratulates me. Everything was left behind: The fight, our "opposing forces," our different languages, and our distinct objectives. We live in a situation different from the previous one. We can talk, understand one another, and who knows, maybe even be friends. Thus the following proverb: Make of your enemy an ardent and faithful friend. Finally he embraces me, says goodbye and wishes me luck. I reciprocate. He will continue forming a part of the mystery of the cave and I will form a part of the mystery of life and of the world. We are "opposing forces" who have found each other. This is my goal in this book: to reunite the "opposing forces." I keep walking in the gallery that gives access to the first scenario. I feel confident and totally calm unlike when I first walked into the cave. Fear, darkness and the unforeseen all scared me. The three doors which signified happiness, fear and failure helped me to evolve and understand the sense of things. Failure represents everything that we run away from without knowing why. Failing must always be a moment of learning. This is the point at which the human being discovers that it is not perfect, that the path is still not drawn and this is the moment of reconstruction. This is what we should always do: Be reborn. Take for example trees: They lose their leaves, but not their life. Let us be as they are: Walking metamorphoses. Life requires this. Fear is present whenever we feel threatened or oppressed. It is the starting point for new failures. Overcome your fears and discover that they only exist in your imagination. I've covered a good part of the gallery of the cave and at this very moment, I pass through the door of happiness. Everyone can go through this door and convinced themselves that happiness exists and can be achieved if we're completely in tune with the universe. It is relatively simple. The worker, the bricklayer, the janitor are happy to fulfill their missions; The farmer, the sugar cane planter, the cowboy are all happy to collect the product of their labor; the teacher in teaching and learning; the writer in writing and reading; the priest proclaiming the divine message, and needy children, orphans, and beggars are happy in receiving words of affection and care. Happiness is within us and expects continuously to be discovered. To be truly happy we should forget hatred, gossip, failures, fear and shame. I keep walking and I see all the traps I managed and wonder what people are made of if they don't have beliefs, paths or destinies. None of them would have survived the traps because they do not have a safety net, a light or force that supports them. Man is nothing if he is alone. He only makes something of himself when he is connected to the forces of humanity. He can only make his place if he is in full harmony with the universe. That is how I feel now: In full harmony because I went up the mountain, I won the three challenges and I beat the cave, the cave that made my dream come true. My walk is nearing its end because I see light coming from the entrance of the cave. Soon I will be out of it.

The Reunion with the Guardian

I am out of the cave. The sky is blue, the sun is strong and the wind is northwest. I begin to contemplate the entire outside world and understand just how beautiful and extensive the universe really is. I feel like an important part of it because I went up the mountain, I performed the three challenges, was tested by the cave and won. I also feel transformed in every way because today I'm no longer just a dreamer but a visionary, blessed with gifts. The cave has really performed a miracle. Miracles happen every day but we do not realize it. A fraternal gesture, the rain which resurrects life, alms, confidence, birth, true love, a compliment, the unexpected, faith moving mountains, luck and destiny; it all represents the miracle that is life. Life is really generous.

I continue to contemplate the exterior, completely in awe. I am connected to the universe and it to me. We are one with the same goals, hopes and beliefs. I am so concentrated that little do I notice when a tiny hand touches my body. I remain in my particular and unique spiritual recollection, until a slight imbalance caused by someone knocks me off my axis. I turn to question and I see a boy and the guardian. I think they have been at my side for quite a while and I didn't realize it.

— So you survived the cave. Congratulations! I was hoping you would. Among all the warriors who already tried to enter into the cave and realize their dreams, you were the most capable. However, you should know that the cave is only one step among many that you will face in life. Knowledge is what will give you true power and this is something that no one will be able to take from you. The challenge is launched. I am here to help you. See here, I brought you this child to accompany you in your true journey. He will be of great help. Your mission is to reunite the "opposing forces" and have them bear fruit at another time. Someone needs your help and therefore I shall send you.

— Thank You. The cave really made my dream come true. Now I am the Seer and am ready for new challenges. What is this true journey? Who is this someone who needs my help? What will happen to me?

— Questions, questions, my dear. I will answer one of them. With your new powers, you will make a trip back in time to distort injustices and help someone find themselves. The rest you will discover for yourself. You have exactly thirty days to carry out this mission. Don't waste your time.

— I understand. When can I go?

— Today. Time is pressing.

That said, the guardian handed me the child and said goodbye amicably. What awaits me on this trip? Could it be that the Seer is really able to fix injustices? I think that all of my powers will be needed to do well on this trip.

Saying Goodbye to the Mountain

The mountain breathes an air of tranquility and peace. Since I came here I have learned to respect it. I think that this also helped me to scale it, to overcome the challenges and to enter into the cave. It really was sacred. It became so due to the death of a mysterious shaman who made a strange pact with the forces of the universe. He promised to give his life in exchange for the restoration of peace in his tribe. For centuries the Xukuru dominated the region. At that time their tribes were at war due to the ruse of a sorcerer from the northern Kualopu tribe. He craved power and total control over the tribes. Their plans also included world domination with their dark arts. Thus began the war. The southern tribe retaliated the attacks and death began. The whole Xukuru nation was threatened to extinction. Then the shaman of the south reunited his forces and made the pact. The southern tribe won the dispute, the wizard was killed, the shaman paid the price of his covenant, and peace was restored. Since then the mountain of Ororubá became sacred.

I am still at the edge of the cave analyzing the situation. I have a mission to accomplish and a boy to look after even though I am not yet a father myself. I analyze the boy from head to toe and immediately I realize it. He is the same child who I tried to save from the claws of that cruel man. It seems to me he is mute because I have yet to hear him speak. I try to break the silence.

— Son, have your parents agreed to let you travel with me? Look, I'm going to take you only if it is strictly necessary.

— I do not have a family. My mother died three years ago. After that, my father took care of me. However, I was abused so much that I decided to escape. The guardian takes care of me now. Remember what she said: You need me on this journey.

— I'm sorry. Tell me: How did your father mistreat you?

— He made me work twelve hours a day. Meals were scarce. I wasn't allowed to play, to study or even to have friends. He beat me frequently. In addition he never gave me any kind of affection that a father should give. So I decided to run away.

— I understand your decision. Despite being a child, you are very wise. You will not suffer anymore with this monster of a father. I promise to take good care of you on this journey.

— Take care of me? I doubt it.

— What is your name?

— Renato. That was the name that the guardian chose for me. Before I didn't have a name or any rights. What is yours?

— Aldivan. But you can call me the Seer or Child of God.

— All right. When will we leave, Seer?

— Soon. Now I need to say my farewells to the mountain.

With a gesture, I made a signal so that Renato would accompany me. I would circle through all the trails and mountain corners before leaving for an unknown destination.

A Journey Back in Time

I have just said my farewells to the mountain. It was important in my spiritual growth and contributed to my knowledge. I will have good memories of it: Its cozy top where I completed the challenges, met the guardian and also where I entered the cave. I cannot forget the ghost, the young girl or the child, who now accompanies me. They were important in the whole process because they made me reflect and critique myself. They contributed to my knowledge of the world. Now I was ready for a new challenge. The mountain's time is over, the cave's as well, and now I will journey back in time. What awaits me? Will I have many adventures? Only time will tell. I'm about to leave the top of the mountain. I take with me my expectations, the bag, my belongings and the boy who won't let go of me. From above, I see the street and its contents in the village of Mimoso. It looks small, but it is important to me because that's where I went up the mountain, won the challenges, entered the cave and met the guardian, the ghost, the young girl and the boy. All of this was important in order for me to become the Seer. The Seer, the person who was able to understand the most confused hearts and transcend time and distance to help others. The decision was made. I would leave.

I take the child's arm firmly and begin to concentrate. A cold wind hits, the sun heats up a little and the voices of the mountain begin to act. Then at the bottom I hear a faint voice calling for help. I focus on this voice and start to use my powers to try to find it. It's the same voice that I heard in the cave of despair. It is the voice of a woman. I am able to create a circle of light around me to protect us from the impacts of traveling through time. I begin to accelerate our speed. We have to achieve the speed of light in order to break through the time barrier. The air pressure increases little by little. I feel dizzy, lost and confused. For a moment, I trespass worlds and planes parallel to our own. I see unjust societies and tyrants as in our own. I see the world of the spirits and observe how they work in the perfect planning of our world. I see fire, light, darkness and curtains of smoke. Meanwhile, our speed accelerates even more. We are close to exceeding the speed of light. The world turns and for a moment I see myself in an old Chinese empire, working on a farm. Another second passes and I am in Japan, serving snacks to the Emperor. Quickly I change locations and I am in a ritual, in Africa, at an Orishan worship session. I continue to relive lives continuously in my memory. The speed increases even more and in a brief moment we have reached ecstasy. The world stops rotating, the circle disbands and we fall to the ground. The journey back in time was complete.

Where am I?

I wake up and realize that I am alone. What happened to Renato? Could it be that he did not survive the time travel? Well, that was all that I could conclude at that moment. Wait? Where am I? I do not know this place. There is no ground, there is no sky, and it is a complete vacuum. A little further away from the place in which I am, I perceive a meeting of people in procession, all dressed in black. I approach them to find out what it is about. I don't like being in unknown places alone. Upon getting closer, I realize that this is not exactly a procession, but a funeral. The coffin stands at the very center sustained by three people. I go up to one of the people who are in attendance.

— What is happening? Whose burial is this?

— What is being buried is the faith and hope of these people.

— What? How?

Without being able to understand it, I walk away from the funeral. What were those crazy people doing? As far as I knew, you buried the dead and not feelings. Faith and hope should never be buried even if it's a desperate situation. The burial disappears in the horizon. The sun appears and an intense light can be seen at the top of the plain. The light is penetrating and consumes my entire being. I forget all troubles, sorrows and sufferings. It is the vision of the Creator and I feel completely relaxed and confident in his presence. In the plane below a shadow surges and with it, evildoers. The vision of darkness embitters me. The two separate plains represent the "opposing forces" which one faces continuously in the universe. I am on the side of good and I will work hard to ensure that it will always prevail. The two plains disappear from my vision and only the empty space remains with me now. The ground appears, the blue sky shines and in an instant, I wake up, as if everything was nothing more than a dream.

First Impressions

The true awakening leaves me in good humor. The trip in time seems to have been a success. At my side, still asleep, I find Renato seeming as if he really enjoyed the journey. Where am I? In a few moments I will find out. I carefully contemplate the place and it looks familiar. The mountains, vegetation, topography, everything is the same. Wait. Something is different. The village no longer seems to be the same. The houses that now exist, spread from one side to the other, if put together in a row would make up no more than one street. I understand what happened: We traveled in time but not in space. I need to come down the mountain to observe all this. I approach Renato and I start to shake him. We can't waste time with delays because we have exactly thirty days to help someone who I still haven't even met. Renato stretches and reluctantly begins to descend the mountain with me. I don't think he has gotten over the battle of time travel yet. He is still a child and needs my care.

We have descended a good part of the route and Mimoso approaches ever-increasingly. Already we can see kids playing in the street, washerwomen with their sacks on a nearby dam, young people socializing in the small local square. What is waiting for us? I wonder who needs help. All these answers will be obtained in the course of the book. Something stands out in the Mimoso sky: Dark clouds fill the entire environment. What does this mean? I'm going to have to find out about it. Our steps accelerate, and we're about one hundred yards from the village. Up north is a towering, stylish, and beautiful home. It must serve as the residence for someone important. In the west, a black castle stands out among the houses. It's scary just by appearance. We finally arrive. We are in the central region where most of the houses are located. I need to find a hotel to rest because the trip was long and tiring. My bags weigh heavy on my arms. I speak with one of the residents who tells me where I can find one. It is a little further south from where we were. We leave to go there.

The Hotel

The journey from where we were up until the hotel was carried out peacefully. We were observed only a little by the people we met. Among these people, some figures stood out: A woman with a hat in the style of Carmen Miranda, a boy with whip marks on his back, and a sad girl accompanied by three strong men who appeared to be her bodyguards. They all acted strangely as if this village wasn't any ordinary community. We are in front of the hotel. On the outside, it can be described like this: A one-story, brick residence, with an area of approximately 1600 square feet with a home-style, inverted, v-shaped roof. The window and the front door are wooden and are covered with fancy curtains. There is a small garden, where flowers of various kinds are growing. This was the only hotel in Mimoso, so we have been informed. Next door, just a few feet away, was a gas station. I was trying to find the bell, but could not. I remembered that we were probably in more ancient times and in addition we were in the countryside where the advances of civilization have not yet arrived. The solution, in order to be attended to, was to use the old method of yelling that awakens even the inveterate deaf.

— Hello! Anybody there?

Before long, the door creaks and thus emerges the figure of a stately woman of about sixty years with light eyes and red hair. She was thin, had flushed cheeks and by analyzing her countenance she is just a little upset.

— What kind of noise is this in my establishment? Have you no manners?

— I'm sorry but it was the only way I could see to get your attention. Are you the owner of the hotel? We'll need accommodation for thirty days. I will pay you generously.

— Yes, I am the owner of this hotel for more than thirty years. My name is Carmen. I only have one room available. Are you interested? The hotel isn't luxurious but it offers good food, friends, regular accommodations and a certain family kind of setting.

— Yes, we'll accept. We're really tired as we have had a long trip. The distance from here to the capital is approximately one-hundred and forty miles.

— Well then, the room is yours. The contractual bases we will figure out later. Welcome. Come on in and relax. Make yourselves at home.

We go through the garden which gives access to the entranceway. Good rest and good food really could recompose our strength. This lady that answered us and whom now we followed was really very nice. The stay at the hotel wouldn't be so monotonous. When she had a little bit of time we could talk and get to know each other better. In addition, I had to find out who I would have to help and what challenges I had to overcome in order to reunite the "opposing forces." This represented another step in my evolution as a clairvoyant.

The door is opened by Carmen and we enter in a small room with furniture characteristically fitting the current time period and decorated with Renaissance paintings. The atmosphere is really very familiar. Sitting on a bench on the right side, are three people. A young man, approximately twenty years old, slender, black eyes and hair and very good looking; A man of some forty years, with a good physique, black hair and brown eyes, a youthful air to him and an engaging smile; and an elderly man, dark-skinned, curly-haired, with a serious attitude and look on his face. Carmen gestured to introduce us:

— This is my husband Gumercindo (pointing to the elderly man), and these are my other guests: Rivanio, (the forty year old), he is known as Vaninho, and is an attendant at the train station and Gomes (the young man), is an employee at the agricultural store.

— My name is Aldivan and this is my nephew, Renato.

With presentations made, Carmen leads us to our room. It is spacious, light and airy. There are two beds in it and this makes me more relaxed. We put away our bags, accommodate ourselves and in that instant Carmen leaves us. We will rest a little and later we'll have dinner.

The Dinner

After a good sleep, I awake with forces renewed. I'm in the hotel room along with Renato. My conscious weighs on me as I realize that I have told lies. I'm not from Recife nor is Renato my nephew. However, it was best. I still don't really know the people to whom I introduced myself. It is better to stay on the defensive because trust is something you earn. On second thought, if I told the truth, they would call me crazy. The truth is that I went up to the mountain in search of my dreams; I performed three challenges and entered the dreaded cave of despair. Dodging traps and scenarios, I became the Seer and I made a trip through time in search of the unknown. Now I was there in search of answers. I get up out of bed, I wake Renato and together we head to the dining room. We were hungry as we haven't eaten for about six hours.

We entered the dining room, greet each other and we sat down. The feast served is varied and is typically Northeastern: Corn porridge with milk or corn meal stew with chicken are the options. For dessert there is cassava dough cake. A conversation starts up and all participate in it.

— Well, Mr. Aldivan, what do you do for a living and what brings you to this tiny place? Questioned Carmen.

— I'm a reporter and journalist in addition to a mathematics teacher. I was sent by the capital's newspaper in order to find a good story. Is it true that this place hides profound mysteries?

— I guess. However, we are forbidden to talk about it. In case you didn't know, we live under the laws and the order of the Empress Clemilda. She is a powerful sorceress who uses dark forces to punish those who disobey. Stay alert: She can hear everything.

For a second, I almost choke on my food. Now I understood the meaning of the dark clouds. The balance of "opposing forces" was broken. This evil woman was blocking the sun's rays, its pure light. This situation could not remain like this for very long otherwise Mimoso could perish along with its inhabitants.

— Is it true that journalists lie a lot? Asks Rivanio.

— That doesn't happen, at least in my case. I try to be faithful to my convictions and to the news. A real journalist is one who is serious, ethical and passionate about their profession.

— Are you married? What are your life goals? Carmen asks.

— No. One time someone told me that God would send someone to me. I am currently focused on my studies and on my dreams. Love will come one day, if it is my destiny.

— Mr. Gumercindo, tell me about Mimoso.

— It's like my wife said, sir, we are forbidden to talk about the tragedy that happened here a few years ago. Since Clemilda began to reign, our lives have not been the same.

Emotion overcame everyone who was in the room. Tears insistently oozed down the face of Gumercindo. This was the face of a poor man who was tired of the cruel dictatorship of this enchantress. Life had lost its meaning to these people. All that was left was for them to die with very little hope that someone would help them.

— Calm down, everyone. It's not the end of the world. This state of being cannot last for very long. The opposing forces of the world should remain in equilibrium. Do not worry. I'll help you.

— How? The witch has powers over humans. Her plagues have destroyed many lives. (Gomes)

— The forces of good are also powerful. They are capable of re-establishing peace and harmony here. Believe me.

My words do not seem to have the desired effect. The conversation changes and I can't concentrate on it. What were these people thinking? God really cared about them. Otherwise, I wouldn't have gone up the mountain, faced the challenges, overcome the cave and met the guardian. All this was a sign that things could change. However, they did not know. Patience was needed to convince them to tell me the truth or at least show me a way. I finish dinner along with Renato. I get up from the table, excuse myself and go to sleep. The next day will be vital in my plans.

A Stroll Through the Village

A new day appears. The sun rises, the birds sing and the freshness of the morning envelopes the entire hotel room that we are in. I wake up feeling awful. Renato is already awake. I stretch, brush my teeth, and take a shower. What I heard the night before makes me slightly concerned. How could Mimoso have been dominated by an evil witch? Under what circumstances? The mystery was too profound for me. Christianity was implemented in the Americas in the sixteenth century and since then it has become supreme, reining the whole continent. Why then, right there, in the middle of nowhere, was evil dominating? I had to find out the causes and the reasons for it.

I leave the room and head to the kitchen to have breakfast. The table is set and I can see some goodies: Manioc, tapioca and potato. I begin to serve myself because I feel at home. The other guests arrive and also act similarly. No one touches the subject of the night before and no one dares to either. Carmen approaches and offers me a cup of tea. I accept. Teas are good for relieving heartache and raising one's spirit. I make conversation with her.

— Could you get someone to guide me while in Mimoso? I would like to do some interviews.

— It's not necessary, my dear. Mimoso is nothing more than a village.

— I'm afraid you misunderstood me. I want someone who's intimate with the people, someone I can trust.

— Well, I can't because I have many duties. All my guests work. I have an idea: Search for Felipe, son of the owner of the Warehouse. He has free time.

— Thanks for the tip. I know where the warehouse is located downtown. I'll call Renato and we'll go together.

— Wonderful. I wish you good luck.

I call for Renato who is still in the hotel room. I hope he'll have breakfast so we can leave. Will I be able to get any accurate information about the case of Mimoso? I was eager to know. Renato finishes his breakfast, we say goodbye to Carmen and finally leave. The plaza adjacent to the hotel is full of young people and children. The young kids are standing around talking with each other and the children are playing. I observe all the excitement while passing by. I turn the corner heading downtown and quickly arrive at the warehouse. A man of about fifty years old is the attendant. I signal for the man to come over.

— How can I help you?

— I'm looking for Felipe. Where he is, please?

— Felipe is my son. Just a moment, I'll call him. He is in the depot.

The man walks away and shortly after returns accompanied by a young redhead, and while skinny is built like a man of about seventeen years old.

— I'm Felipe. What did you need?

— Carmen recommended you to me. I need you to accompany me on some interviews. My name is Aldivan, nice to meet you.

— Sure, my pleasure, I'll accompany you. I have some free time. We can begin with the pharmacy that is next door. The owner is a connoisseur of the place as he's been here since the foundation.

— Great. Let's go.

Accompanied by Renato and Felipe I go to the Pharmacy where I will perform my first interview. The fact that I am not a true journalist makes me a little nervous and anxious. I hope I do well. After all, I went up the mountain, I performed three challenges and I passed the cave's test. A simple interview won't tear me down. Upon arriving at the pharmacy we are attended to promptly. We are introduced to the owner. I ask to interview him and he agrees. We retire to a more appropriate location where we can be alone and talk. I begin the interview shyly.

— Is it true that you are one of the oldest residents, one of the founders of this place?

— Yes, and don't call me Sir. My name is Fabio. Mimoso really began to stand out ever since the implantation of the railroad department. Progress and modern technology arrived in 1909 with the Great Western trains. The British engineers Calander, Tolester and Thompson designed the tracks of the railroad, built the station buildings and Mimoso began to grow. Trade was implemented and Mimoso became one of the largest warehouses in the region, second only to Carabais. Mimoso is destined to grow and that's why I'm here.

— Has life here always been smooth or has it experienced tragic events?

— Yes, it has been. At least up until one year ago. Since then it hasn't been the same. People are sad and have lost all hope. We live under a dictatorship. The tax burden is too high, we don't have freedom of speech and we have to render our votes up to hidden forces. Religion for us has become synonymous with oppression. Our Gods are cruel Gods who want blood and vengeance. We've lost real contact with God the Father, the One and Only.

— Tell me about what happened one year ago.

— I don't want to and I can't even talk about the tragedy. It's very painful.

— Please, I need this information.

— No. My family would suffer if I told you. The spirits can hear everything and would tell Clemilda. I couldn't take so much of a risk.

I insist, again and again, but he becomes adamant. Fear has made him a coward and small-minded. He retires from the place without further explanation. I'm alone, restless and full of questions. Why do they fear this sorceress so much? Of what tragedy did he speak? I needed this information to know on what ground I was standing. I was the Seer, gifted of gifts, but that didn't make it easier. If this Clemilda ruled the dark forces, she would be a formidable adversary. Black magic is capable of capturing any human being even the best natured ones. The clash of the "opposing forces" could destroy the universe and this was the farthest thing from my mind. Caution was needed right now. What was clear to me was that the balance of "opposing forces" was broken and it was my mission to reunite it. But for that it was necessary to know the whole story. I walk away with that thought. I find Renato and Felipe and we leave for new interviews. I hope to succeed.

I'm totally frustrated after the interviews. I didn't get all of the information that I needed. What kind of journalist was I? I think I should have taken a course in journalism. All the persons I interviewed, the baker and blacksmith, repeated what I already knew. Renato and Felipe try to console me but I cannot forgive myself. Now I was lost, at the end of the world where civilization has not yet arrived. The only information I knew was that Mimoso was ruled by an evil witch. The scream that I heard in the cave of despair still made me dizzy. Who was it that needed my help so much? I was concentrating on this cry and, aided by my powers, had come to Mimoso via time travel. The goals of this trip were not yet clear to me. The guardian had spoken of reuniting the "opposing forces" but I had no idea how to do this. What I knew is that I still didn't have full control over my "opposing forces" and that distressed me even more. Well, now was not the time to be discouraged. I still had twenty-eight days to resolve this issue. The best now was to get back to the hotel and gather my strength as I would need it. Renato and Felipe were with me and on the way we got to know each other better. They are really good people. I don't feel so alone in this place that is dominated by the forces below and is full of mysteries.

The Black Castle

We're on our third day after time traveling. The previous day had not left good memories. After the interviews, I decided to spend the rest of the day at the hotel finding myself. This was my starting point: Find myself to resolve important issues. Renato still has not helped me at all so far. I think the guardian was wrong to have sent him with me. After all, he was just a child and as such didn't have many responsibilities. My situation was entirely different. I was a young man of twenty-six, an administrative assistant, with a degree in mathematics and many goals. I didn't have time to think about love or myself because I was on a mission, even though I didn't know exactly what that was. The only certainty that I had was that I went up the mountain, realized the challenges, found the young girl, the ghost, the child and the guardian and I passed the tests within the cave. I became the Seer but that wasn't all. I had to overcome life's challenges continuously. Well, a new day is dawning, and with it new hopes. I get up, take a shower and have breakfast, brush my teeth and say farewell to Carmen. The previous day has awoken in me a new idea: To know my enemy intimately and steal information from them. It was the only way out.

I go out into the street, and see the playground and everyone sitting on the benches. They act normally as if they were in a normal community. They have conformed. Human beings become accustomed to anything even during times of doom. I keep walking. I turn the corner, meet some people and I remain firm in my resolve. The challenges of the cave helped me lose my fear of any kind of circumstance. I found three doors representing fear, failure and happiness. I chose happiness and disposed of the rest. I was ready for new challenges. I turn another corner and come to the west side of the village. A large castle appears. It's an imposing building composed of two main towers and a secondary tower. The residence is black painted brickwork. Bad taste, typical of a villain. My heart races and my steps do so too. The future of Mimoso depended on my attitude. Innocent lives were at stake and I would not allow any more injustices. I clap my hands hoping to get the attention of someone in the house. A robust boy, tall and dark-skinned comes out from inside the house.

— What did you need?

— I'm here to see Clemilda.

— She is busy now. Come another time.

— Wait a moment. It is important. I'm a reporter for the Daily Journal and I've come to do a special report on her. Just give me five minutes.

— Reporters? Well, I think she'll like that. I'll announce your arrival.

— No need. Allow me to come with you.

The man signals "yes" and I start up the numerous steps that give access to the front door. A shiver runs through my body and insistent voices warn me not to go in. A cat walks past and flashes its fierce claws. I pray inwardly that God gives me the strength to withstand any situation. The boy accompanies me, and we go in. The door gives access to a large ornate foyer filled with colors and life. On the right side, there is access to over three more chambers. In the center are images of saints with horns, skulls and other sinful objects. On the left side are strange paintings. The scenario is horrific and I can't fully describe it. Negative forces dominate the place and make me dizzy as this is a clash of the "opposing forces." The man stops in front of one of the compartments and knocks. The door opens, smoke rises and a fat, black woman with strong features, about forty years old, appears.

— To what do I owe the honor of the Seer in person coming to visit me?

She signals for the man to disappear. I am completely perplexed by her attitude. How did she know me? Could it be that she knew about the mountain and the cave? What strange powers did that woman possess? This and many other questions passed through my mind at that moment.

— I see you know me. Then you should know why I came here. I want to know about the tragedy and how you've dominated over such a quiet place.

— Tragedy? What tragedy? Nothing happened here. I have only modified the place a bit to make it become more enjoyable. People with their fake happiness... they got on my nerves and I decided to change it. Mimoso became my property and not even you can do anything about it. Your psychic powers are nothing compared to mine.

— Every villain is smug and proud. We both know that this situation cannot continue for long. The "opposing forces" must remain in equilibrium in the entire universe. Good and evil cannot oppose each other because otherwise the universe is at risk of disappearing.

— I don't care about the universe or its people! They're nothing but insects. Mimoso is my domain and you must respect that. If you oppose me, you will suffer. I just need to mention one word to the major and I'll have you arrested.

— Are you threatening me? I'm not afraid of threats. I am the Seer who went up the mountain, completed three challenges and beat the cave.

— Get out of here, before I cook you in my cauldron. I'm sick of your virtue. It disgusts me.

— I will go, but we will meet again. Good always prevails in the end.

Very quickly, I leave her and walk to the door. As I leave, I still hear her jests. She's really quite mad. My questions remain unanswered, and I remain aimless and without any signs. The meeting with Clemilda had not fulfilled my goal.

The Chapel Ruins

Upon leaving the black castle, I decide to take another path. I want to see some more of the town and its people. Walking towards the east, I find some and try to make conversation. However, they avoid me. Their mistrust is even greater because I am an unknown, young reporter. They don't know my true intentions. I want to save Mimoso, find the person I'm looking for and reunite the "opposing forces" as the guardian asked of me. But for that it was necessary to borrow a bit from the history of the place and know exactly all of my enemies. I would have to find all of that out as soon as possible because I had a deadline to meet. The ascent of the mountain, the challenges, the cave, all this was necessary knowledge for me to know what life was like and how people were living it. It was time to put it into practice. I turn around the corner and a few feet ahead I come across a pile of rubble. I think about the lack of organization of the place and its people. Trash floating freely among society and being able to transmit diseases and serve as an animal and insect nursery; this was harmful to man. I get closer for a better look at the calamity of the place. Wait. There's something different in this garbage. Semi-dug up, I see a huge wooden crucifix as if it were from a chapel. I move the garbage around better and can see clearly: It is a crucifix. Upon touching it, a wave of heat courses through my whole body and I begin to have visions. I see blood, suffering and pain. For a moment, I find myself at that location participating in events of the past. I take my hand off of the crucifix. I'm not ready yet. I need some time to absorb everything I've felt in less than three seconds. The cross somehow enhances my powers and I'm starting to feel the action of a force opposing mine.

The Order

My visit to the dreaded, dark sorceress named Clemilda hadn't left her happy. She had never been contradicted. Her domain over the community of Mimoso was completely unrestricted. However, she hadn't counted on the strength of good sending me on a trip back in time to the place. Immediately after my departure from the castle, she reunited with her lackeys, Totonho and Cleide and they consulted the occult forces. They entered in the left compartment located in the hall and took, as a sacrifice, a small pig. The witch took a book and began to recite satanic prayers in another language and she and her cronies began to sacrifice the poor animal. A trail of blood filled the compartment and the negative forces began to concentrate. The natural lighting of the area was dimmed and the sorceress began to scream crazily. In a short time, darkness took over the enclosure and a door of communication between the two worlds was opened through a mirror. Clemilda performed with reverence to her Lord and began to refer to him. She was the only one on that compound that had this ability. The sinful oracle and her receptor were at full communion for some time. The others just watched the whole situation. After the meeting, the darkness dissipated and the site returned to its initial state. Clemilda regained herself from the impact of the conversation, called her helpers and told them:

— Spread throughout the community the following order: Whoever, man or woman, gives any information to a man named the Seer will be severely punished. His or her death will be tragic and will mark their passage into the realm of darkness. This is the order of the Queen Clemilda for all of Mimoso.

Hastily Clemilda's lackeys went to fulfill the order of announcing the news to the residents of the village, to neighboring sites and to the farmlands.

Meeting of Residents

With the order issued by Clemilda, the residents were even more reticent on the matter. Fabio, the pharmacy owner and president of the homeowners' association, called an urgent meeting with the main leaders of the place. The meeting was scheduled at 10:00 AM in the association building downtown. They would deliberate on my case.

At the appointed time, the main hall of the building was entirely filled. Present were Major Quintino, the delegate Pompeu, Osmar (farmer), Sheco (owner of the warehouse), and Otavio (the agricultural store owner), among others. Fabio, the president, began the session:

— Well, my friends, as you are all aware, Clemilda released an order yesterday afternoon. No one should pass on any information to a subject called "the Seer" who's staying at the hotel. I see that this individual is very dangerous and must be contained. He even tried to gather some information from me but failed. He wanted to know about the tragedy.

— The Seer? I haven't heard of this person. Where does he come from? Who is he? What does he want with our little village? (Asked the major)

— Easy, Major. We still do not know that. The only information we have is that he is a mysterious outsider. We need to decide what to do with him. (Fabio)

— Wait minute, guys. From what I know he's not a criminal. My son Felipe accompanied him on a walk to town and told me that he is a good, honest person. (Sheco)

— Appearances can be deceiving, son. If Clemilda has laid this order upon us, then this man has become a danger to us. We will need to banish him as soon as possible. (Otavio)

— If you need my services, I'm available. (Pompeu, the delegate)

A minor disturbance occurs in the assembly. Some begin to protest. Pompeu gets up, consults the major and says:

— Let's arrest this man. In prison we will ask all of the necessary questions of him.

The group disassembles with the order to arrest me. Could it be that I was a criminal?

Decisive Conversation

I leave the chapel ruins and start walking toward the hotel. My sixth sense tells me that I'm in danger. In fact, since I've been in Mimoso it has always warned me about where I was going. A village dominated by the dark forces was not a good choice of vacation. However, I would have to fulfill the promise made to the guardian of the mountain: To reunite the "opposing forces" and to help the owner of that scream that I heard in the cave of despair. I couldn't ever abandon this mission. My footsteps accelerate and soon I arrive at the hotel. I open the door, go to the kitchen and find Carmen, my last hope. I felt enough courage and counted on kindness to help me.

— Ms. Carmen, I need to speak with you ma'am.

— Tell me, Aldivan, what do you want?

— I want to know everything about the tragedy and history of Mimoso.

— My son, I can't. Don't you know the latest? Clemilda threatened to kill all those who give information to you.

— I know. She is a snake. However, if you don't help me, Mimoso will sink even more and run the risk of disappearing.

— I do not believe it. The rotten never perish. That's the lesson I've learned since she began to reign.

Silence prevailed for a few moments and I realized that if I didn't tell the truth, I would not have any answers. My captors were preparing to attack.

— Carmen, listen carefully to what I'm going to say. I'm neither a journalist nor a reporter. Actually, I am a time traveler whose mission it is to restore the balance that Mimoso so greatly needs. Before I came here, I went up the mountain of Ororubá;

I performed three challenges, found a young man, the guardian, the ghost and Renato. Overcoming the challenges, I obtained the right to enter the cave of despair, the cave which can realize even the most profound dreams. In the cave, I avoided traps and advanced through scenarios which no other human being has ever surpassed. The cave made me the Seer, a being able to transcend time and distance to resolve grievances. With my new powers, I was able to travel back in time and arrive here. I want to reunite the "opposing forces," help someone I don't know and overthrow the tyranny of this wicked witch. In the end, I need to know everything and know what you're capable of revealing. You're a good person and like the others here you deserve to be free as God created us.

Carmen sat down in a chair and became emotional. Copious tears were sliding down under her face that was mature from suffering. I held her hands and our eyes met in an instant. For a moment, I felt as if I was in the presence of my own mother. She got up and motioned for me to accompany her. We stopped in front of a door.

— You will find the answers that you greatly need right here in this depository. It is what I can do for you: Show you the way. Good luck!

I thank her and give her a blessed crucifix. She smiles. I enter the storage room, close the door and I come across a multitude of printed newspaper. Where would this thing that I am looking for be?

Vision

I sit on the only chair available, support myself on the small table and start flipping through the newspapers I find. All are from the period 1909-1910. I read only the headlines, but they don't seem to have much to do with what I'm looking for. Some talk about Pesqueira and other municipalities in the region but the issues addressed refer to issues of health, education and politics. What am I really looking for? A tragedy that was able to shake this little place and make it a field of darkness. I keep flipping through the papers and it seems to me that this will be a tiresome and monotonous task. Why didn't Carmen just tell me directly? Wasn't I trustworthy? It would be much simpler. Again I remember the mountain, the challenges and the cave. Not always was the simplest way easier, clearer, or more palpable. I'm starting to understand it a little. After all, she was under the power of a vile, cruel and arrogant witch. She showed me the way, exactly how she said and I think that this would be enough for me to win, accomplish my goals and be happy. I keep flipping through the papers and pick up a pouch of ones from 1910. If I remembered correctly, that was the year of the tragedy as Fabio had informed me in the interview. I begin to read the headlines and the news. I had to check all possibilities.

After an hour of reading and rereading the newspapers I hadn't found anything that called my attention. Rural news, sports and other sections was all I could find. The hope that I had of finding the news was in this 1910 paper pouch that I took. Wait. If this tragedy really happened, it certainly should be in a newspaper which had been especially separated, since this was such big news. I start searching the drawers of the cabinet next to the table. I find various newspapers with different dates. One strikes me: It's from the day of the 10th of January

1910 and has the following headline: Christine, the Young Monster. I think I found what I was looking for. Upon touching the paper, a cold wind hits me, my heart races and like a trip through time I experience the vision of this history.

The Beginning

The twentieth century began and with it the emergence of the first pioneers of the land located west of Pesqueira. The first who went were the Major Quintino and his friend Osmar both originating in the State of Alagoas and who appropriated lands that was the property of the natives. The natives were kicked out, humiliated and murdered. The two decided not to move permanently to the region since it had no structure suitable for them.

Over time, there came other people who cleared lots for the mayor's office. The land was donated and the first houses built. Thus arose a settlement. The settlement attracted some traders in the region interested in expanding their businesses. A warehouse, a gas station, a grocery store, a pharmacy, a hotel and an agricultural shop were opened. An elementary school was built to serve as the intellectual basis for the general population. Mimoso then moved to the category of village subject to Pesqueira's headquarters.

The Railroad

From 1909, Great Western trains arrived in Mimoso bringing progress and technology to the peaceful place. British engineers Calander, Tolester and Thompson were responsible for laying the rails and the construction of the station buildings. The European influence can also be observed in other buildings' masonry and in the urban areas of Mimoso.

With the implementation of the railway, Mimoso (the name comes from Mimoso grass, very common in the region) became a center of commercial importance and regional political relevance. Strategically located on the border of the hinterlands with the wilderness, the village was consolidated as a point of arrival and departure of the products from many municipalities of Pernambuco, Paraíba and Alagoas. In addition to the railroad, the dirt road linking Recife to the wilderness passed exactly at its center, contributing to the progress of the place.

The population of Mimoso was formed basically by the descendants of families of Lusitanian origin. The least favored part of the population were the descendants of Indian and African origin. The people of Mimoso can be characterized as a friendly and welcoming people.

The Move

With the consolidation of the implementation of the railway and the consequent progress in Mimoso, the pathfinders of the region (the farmers, Major Quintino and Osmar) decided to take up residence on site with all of their respective families.

It was the 10th day of February, 1909. The weather was nice, the wind was North-East and the aspect of the village as normal as possible. A train appears on the horizon directed by engineer Roberto bringing the new local habitants from Recife: Major Quintino, his wife, Helena, his only daughter Christine and their maid Gerusa, a black woman from Bahia. Inside the train, in the passenger compartment, a restless Christine reveals herself.

— Mother, it looks like we're arriving. What will Mimoso be like? Will I like it?

— Hush, my child. Do not be so anxious. Soon you will find out. The important thing is that we're together as a family. Before long, we'll settle in and make friends.

The major watches the two and decides to join the conversation.

— You need not worry. You will not lack anything. I have built a beautiful house located in one of the lands that I own. It is next to the village. Remember: You will have full freedom to relate to people of our social level but I don't want you to have contact with the unclean or the very poor.

— That's prejudice, Daddy! At the nunnery where I stayed for three years I was taught to respect every human being regardless of social class, ethnicity or race, belief or religion. We are worth what we hold within our hearts.

— Those nuns are disconnected from reality because they live cloistered. I should not have allowed you to go there because you've come back with a head full of nonsense. Ideas of your mother, to whom I no longer listen.

— I always dreamed that she became a nun. Christine was for me a great gift from God. I taught her all the precepts of the religion that I knew. When she turned fifteen, I sent her to the nunnery because I was sure of her vocation. However, three years later, she gave up and it still hurts a lot. It was one of the biggest disappointments that she ever gave me.

— It was your dream, Mother, and not mine. There are infinite ways to serve God. It is not necessary for me to be a nun to understand Him and to understand his Will.

— Of course not! -I'm going to arrange a good marriage for her. I already have some ideas. Well, now is not the time for me to reveal.

The train whistles signaling that it will stop. The village emerges; Christine sees all of the rural aspects of the place through one of the windows. Her heart tightens and she feels a slight shudder in her body. Her thoughts fill with doubt with that premonition. What waited for her in Mimoso? Keep with us, reader.

Christine and Helen, with their hoop skirts, squeeze out of the exit door of the train. The major doesn't like it. The four exit and cause a certain spark of curiosity from the other local residents. They behave with elegance and opulence. The major greets Rivanio as a courtesy. From then on, they depart for their home, which is located in the north of the village.

The Arrival at the Bungalow

Christine, the Major, Helena and Gerusa arrive at their new home. It is a brick and mortar house, bungalow style, some 1600 square feet of constructed area, that's surrounded by a garden of fruit trees. Inside there are two living areas, four bedrooms, a kitchen, a laundry area and a bathroom. On the outside there are maid's quarters with a room and bathroom. The four walk in silence until the major speaks up.

— Well here it is, our house that I built a few months ago. I hope you like it. It is spacious and comfortable.

— It looks very nice. I think we're going to be happy here. (Helena)

— I also hope so, despite the premonition that I just had. (Christine)

— Premonitions are nonsense. You will be happy, my daughter. This place is nice, filled with good and hospitable people. (Major)

The four enter the house. They unpack their bags and get some rest. The trip had been long and tiring. Beginning another day, they would fully explore the place.

Meeting with the Mayor

A new day arises and Mimoso presents itself with the aspects of any rural community. Farmers come out of their homes and prepare for a new day of toil, trade officials do so as well. Children pass by with their mothers in the direction of the newly founded school. The donkeys circulate normally carrying their loads and people. Meanwhile, in the beautiful bungalow, the major prepares to leave. He was heading to a meeting in Pesqueira, with the mayor. Helena gently straightens his jacket.

— This meeting is very important to me, wife. Important lords of the land are to be there, such as the Colonel of Carabais. I have to reaffirm my place over Mimoso.

— You're going to do fine as you are the only one in this place with the rank of Major in the National Guard. It was a good idea to buy that position.

— Of course it was. I am a man of vision and strategy. Since I left Alagoas and came here, I have only had victories.

— Don't forget to ask for a position for our daughter Christine. She has been doing little to nothing. The education that she received in the convent is enough for her to perform any duties.

— You need not worry. I will know how to persuade him. Our daughter is intelligent and deserves a good job. Well, I must go. I don't want to be late to the meeting.

With a kiss, the major says goodbye to his wife, Helena. He walks towards the door, opens it and leaves. His thoughts concentrate on the arguments he will use at the hearing. He thinks of the power, glory and social ostentation which his rank of major will give him. He dreams big. He dreams of becoming the Governor's friend and by doing so, getting more favors. After all, all that mattered to him was power, and his daughter's future, of course. Others became mere pawns in his game. He picks up the pace for in five minutes the train to Pesqueira will depart. For a moment, he turns his attention to the poor people he sees on the way. He regrets it and turns his face to the other side. A major can't mingle with everyone, he thinks. The most humble and excluded, for him, only count at election time. When that moment passes, they lose their value and after that the major does not pay any more attention to their demands or needs. The poor, under control of the Colonels, are uneducated and resigned. The major keeps walking and approaches the train station. When he arrives, he buys a ticket and boards quickly.

On the train, he looks for the best seat and begins to remember his childhood. He was a poor boy, from a suburb of Maceió, who worked as a candy salesman. He remembers humiliations and punishments by his father and the fights with his older brothers. These were times he wanted to forget but his memory stubbornly refused to stop reminding him. His strongest memory is of the fight with his stepmother and of the knife he wielded to kill her. Blood gushing, screams, cries and him escaping from home after the act come to mind. He becomes a beggar and shortly thereafter is introduced to drugs, alcoholism and delinquency. He sinks into that world for about five years until one day, a pious woman appears and adopts him. He grows, becomes a man and meets Helena, a farmer's daughter, with whom he marries. Some time after, they have their first and only daughter, Christine. They move to Recife. He purchases the rank of Major of the National Guard and travels deep into the interior looking for land. He conquers everything from the western side all the way to Pesqueira. He takes over the lands and becomes a very powerful man who is well-known and respected. He felt himself a grand man in every way. Life had taught him to be a strong, calculating and conquering man. He would use all of these weapons to achieve his goals. Still on the train he notices right behind him, a woman with a child on her lap. He remembers Christine and her innocence and sweetness when she was small. He also remembers the birthday gift he gives Christine, a rag doll. He gives her the present; she embraces him and calls him dear father. He gets emotional but can't cry because men can't do that in public. His little Christine was now a beautiful and attractive young lady. He would need to arrange a good marriage and some duties for her. Thinking about it he falls asleep in a restorative nap. The train sways; he wakes up and queries his pocket watch to see what time it is. He notes that it is close to the time of the meeting. The train accelerates; Pesqueira comes into view and his heart calms. His mind is now concentrated on the meeting and he is thinking about the encounter with his farmer friends. The train signals that it will stop and the major stands to expedite his way out. Life required sacrifices and he more than anyone else knew that. The time during his boyhood and his life experiences qualified him even more. The train finally stops and he hurries down towards the city's political headquarters.

It's 8:00 AM and the gigantic building is already completely filled. The major enters, greets the people he knows and sits in one of the front seats reserved for him. The session has not yet begun. A loud racket is heard throughout the general headquarters. Some complain of the delay, others about their relatives who could not all fit into the mayor's office. The building manager tries in vain to control the situation. Finally the mayor's secretary arrives, asks for silence and all obey. He announces:

— His Excellency, Mayor Horacio Barbosa, will address you now.

The mayor enters, straightens his clothes and prepares to give a speech.

— Good morning, my dear compatriots. It is with great satisfaction that I welcome you to this seat that represents the power and strength of our municipality. It is with great joy that I called you here to talk a little bit about our municipality and empowering the political representatives of Mimoso and Carabais. Our municipality has been growing a lot in the commercial sector and in agriculture. On the border of the wilderness with the hinterlands, we have Mimoso as the main trading post. We have your political representative, Major Quintino, present here. In the hinterlands we have Carabais, and with its familiar farming it has managed to render many dividends for the city. The Colonel of Carabais, Mr. Soares, is also here. The tourism of our municipality is also developing after the establishment of the railroad. As you can see, our municipality is growing..............................

....

....

....

....

..... Finally, I would like to please introduce Mr. Soares and Mr. Quintino. Let us applaud them.

The assembly stands and applauds them both.

— With my authority as mayor, I now pronounce you commanders of your respective localities. Your function is to rule, with an iron fist, the interests of the public, oversee the collection of taxes, and maintain law and justice conforming to our interests. I promise to help you in every way.

Sashes are awarded to them and all clap. Quintino signals for the mayor and both withdraw from the podium. They would have a private conversation. The two enter a restricted room.

— Well, Your Excellency, I asked for a moment of your time because I have two questions to deliberate with you. First, I want a higher percentage on tax collections. Second, a job for my daughter, Christine. As you know, Mimoso became a trading post of great importance after the railroad and with that, the profits of the prefecture proportionally increased. I want then to become stronger and more powerful and who knows, to even be your successor. In addition, I want a good job and a good salary for my daughter, Christine. She's been rather...static lately.

— With respect to profits, your question becomes impossible. The city has many expenses and my administration is transparent and serious. Personally, I can do nothing. As for the job, who knows, I can give her the teaching position.

— How so? Your administration is transparent and serious? The corruption here is notorious! Remember well that I supported your governor and got him a considerable percentage of the vote. If you don't give me what I'm asking for, the support is off.

The mayor was quiet, and thought and rethought about his office. He set his eyes on Quintino and commented.

— You really are terrible. I don't want to be one of your enemies. Very well. I will increase your percentage and I will give the post of tax collector to your daughter. How's that?

A slight smile filled the face of Major Quintino. His arguments had been enough to convince the mayor. He really was a winner and a warrior.

— Very well. I accept. Thank you for understanding, Your Excellency.

Quintino said goodbye and retreated from the room. The meeting was adjourned and all withdrew from the hall.

Meeting of Farmers

After the end of the hearing, the main "Gentlemen" of the city of Pesqueira gather in a bar close to where they had been. Among them, the Colonel of Sanharó (Mr. Goncalves), the Colonel of Carabais (Mr. Soares) and Major Quintino, of Mimoso. They talk cheerfully about power, strength and prestige.

— The implementation of the railway was the trump card of the government. It encouraged production and the marketing of our wealth. Pesqueira already highlights at the state level. Its districts have become referenced in many different genres. Mimoso, for example, became a very important commercial strategic spot. I can already see all of the benefits that I will be able to take advantage of in this situation. Wealth, social ostentation, political power and unrestricted command. My enemies will have no respite for I will deal with them with iron and fire. My team is already prepared for the rebels. (Major Quintino)

— As for Carabais, the railroad did not affect our finances simply because of the fact that it does not cut through our district. The government technicians saw fit to divert it just before the entrance of the village. The soil was not suitable for the deployment of rails. Our district, though, is an important agricultural hub. Our products are exported to neighboring states. As Colonel, I dominate the region and I am respected. Those who are enemies of mine will not survive for very long.

— The establishment of the railroad in Sanharó was important but not the only source of income. The agriculture is strong and we excel at the state level. Our milk and our meats are first class and give us good yields. As for my enemies I treat them the same way as you. We need to maintain the power of the Colonel System.

— That is true. This system should be maintained for our own good. Rigging votes, fraud, the network of favors...all this benefits us. Our power and our strength come from torture, pressure and intimidation. Brazil is this: A great power structure where only the strongest survive. From the southeast, where the rich coffee growers dominate, to the northeastern parts run by Colonels, the system is the same. Only the names and situations change. We have to keep the people quiet and resigned as this is the best for our ambitions and goals. (Major)

— I fully agree and in order to keep the people quiet and agreeable it is necessary to maintain our acts of cruelty, oppression and authoritarianism. The people should fear us. Otherwise, we lose respect and our benefits. The world is unfair and we should be part of the small part of the population that are the winners. To win it is necessary to kill, humiliate and take down precepts and values and that is what we will do. (Coronel of Carabais)

The conversation continues excitedly about women, hobbies and other matters. They spend close to two hours talking. Major Quintino rises, says goodbye to the others and leaves. The train that goes to Pesqueira-Mimoso was soon leaving.

Back Home

The major rushes back towards Pesqueira's rail station. The train is stationary waiting for the exact moment to leave. He goes to the ticket office, buys the ticket, leaves a tip and heads toward the train. He boards, complains about the delay of the collector to serve him and sits down. The train signals that it's leaving and the major focuses on his plans. He sees himself as Mayor of Pesqueira, right-hand man of the governor and grandfather of at least five grandchildren. Christine's children with a son-in-law that he would choose. After all, a man is achieved only if he can marry off his children. The train leaves and takes along with it the dreaming major.

The rhythm of the train is quite regular. The passengers sit calm and comfortably. An employee offers juices and snacks to passengers. The major takes a snack, chews and imagines how good the taste of victory and success is. He had gone to a meeting and had come back with his plans implemented. He would be entitled to a higher percentage of taxes and a good job for his daughter. What more could he want? He was a made man, happy in his marriage and had a beautiful daughter. He held the rank of Major of the National Guard, which he had bought, and that gave him the right to politically dominate Mimoso. The only thing that would make him happier would be if he was Colonel, the Governor's right-hand man and married his daughter off to an ideal son-in-law. This would definitely happen. Time passes and the train gets closer to the small town of Mimoso, his electoral corral. He was eager to break the news to the two women in his life. His heart speeds up and a cold wind hits his body as suddenly the train changes its pace. It's probably nothing, he thinks to himself. The rhythm of the train goes back to normal and he calms down. Mimoso is approaching closer and closer. For a moment, he thinks that the world could be fairer and that all should be winners just as he was. He attempts to deviate from this thought. He learned since childhood what life was like and knew it wouldn't change from one minute to the next. He still bore the marks of his suffering: His father's punishments, the fight with his older brothers, the murder he had committed. His brain kept those memories intact from that era. If he could, he would toss those memories in the garbage, far, far away. The train whistles signaling that it will stop. Passengers fix their hair and clothes. The train passes and everyone gets off, including the major. The arrival is relaxed and he is all smiles. After all, he came back from Pesqueira victorious.

The Announcement

Upon getting off the train, the major heads to the station, says hello to Rivanio and asks if everything is okay. He replies yes and the major bids farewell and leaves for his house. Along the way, he meets some people and they talk about education. He hurries his steps and in a few minutes is near his residence. Upon arriving, he enters without ceremony, and finds Gerusa cleaning house and sends her to call the two women in his life. They arrive and hug and kiss him. The major asks that they sit and they obey promptly.

— I just came from the meeting I had in Pesqueira and the news couldn't be better. First, I will receive a higher percentage on the taxes that I collect. Second, I got the job of tax collector for my beloved daughter Christine. What do you think?

— Sensational. I am proud to be the wife of a man with true character such as you. We will only become richer and more powerful as time progresses.

— I'm happy for you, Daddy. Don't you think that the job of tax collector is a bit masculine for me?

— Aren't you happy, daughter? It's a great job and with adequate remuneration. I don't think it's a man's job. It is a position of high trust that only you can perform.

— Of course it's a great job. As her mother, I approve unreservedly.

— OK. You have convinced me. When do I begin?

— Tomorrow. Your function is to monitor and enforce the official tax collector, Claudio, son of Paulo Pereira, owner of the gas station. He is responsible and honest but it's like the story says, opportunity makes the man.

— I think it will be good for me. It's a great opportunity to meet people and make friends.

The major retires and goes to take a bath. Christine goes back to the knitting that she was doing before her father arrived and Helena goes to give orders to the kitchen maid. The next day would be her first day on the job.

The First Day of Work

A new day begins. The sun is shining, the birds are singing and the morning breeze envelopes the bungalow. Christine had just woken up after a deep and revitalizing sleep. The dream she had the night before had left her deeply intrigued. She dreamed of the convent and the nuns who she learn to admire during the three years of her life devoted to religion. They participated in her wedding. What did that mean? It wasn't in her plans to marry at that time. She was young, free and full of plans. Her sense of self-protection cried out inside her. No, she really wasn't ready for marriage. She stretches quietly in her bed and looks at the time. It was close to 6:30 AM. She gets up, yawns and goes to the bathroom of the suite. She goes in, turns on the faucet and the cold water carries her to her convent times. She remembers the gardener who worked there and his son who had captivated her. They began romantic games and took walks together and in no time she had discovered that she was in love. Her contact continued with the gardener's son but one day one of the nuns caught them kissing. The Mother Superior was consulted, Christine's bags were packed and she was expelled from the convent. On this day she felt a great relief. Relief of no longer lying to herself or to life itself. The contact with the gardener's son was disbanded; she forgets him and leaves for home. Her mother and father greet her at home with surprise. She disappointed her mother and gave new hope to her father who wanted to see her married with children. Time passed and she hadn't fallen in love since. She learned to knit and embroider to better pass the time. Now she was employed as tax collector by her father's influence. She felt anxious and nervous about the new situation. She turns off the cold water, soaps up and begins to imagine her new coworker, Claudio. She pictures a tall, blond boy, full of tattoos. She likes what she sees and continues bathing. She cleans her body roughly as if she was taking out impurities from her very soul. She turns off the faucet and puts on two towels: A larger one on her body and a smaller one on her head. She walks out of the suite and goes to the kitchen to have breakfast. She sits, serves herself some cake, and greets her father and mother. The major begins to make conversation.

— Are you excited, my daughter? I hope you do well on your first day of work. You will learn a lot from Claudio. He is a great tax collector.

— Yes, I am. I can't wait to get to work because knitting and embroidery aren't as fun as they used to be. This work will serve me well although I think it's a little masculine.

— Again, with this? Can't you see that you hurt your father with these insinuations? He does everything for you.

— Excuse me, both of you. I'm a little stubborn with some ideas.

Christine finishes her breakfast, says goodbye with a kiss on the foreheads of her parents and walks to the door. She opens it and heads to the gas station. Along the way doubts assault her: Will this Claudio act like caveman? Will he respect her at work? She knew nothing about him except that he was Pereira's son and had two sisters: Fabiana and Patricia. She keeps walking and as soon as she approaches the gas station she feels even more anxious and nervous. She stops and breathes a little. She seeks inspiration in the universe, in nature and in her troubled heart. She remembers the lessons she learned in the convent, the nuns and their distinct way of seeing life. It was a three year period of spiritual gathering that seemed to have no meaning now. She was at the point of meeting new people, starting a new craft and who knows if this wouldn't change her way of seeing people and life. That's what she would find out as time went on. She continues to walk. A new force refreshes her and fills her being and gives her an extra push. She had to be brave as during the time she faced the Mother Superior of her convent and confessed the truth. That she was completely in love. They packed her bags, she was kicked out and at that point it felt as if they had taken a huge weight off of her back. She relocated from the capital and was now residing at the end of the world without friends and without any comforts. She would have to get used to it. A few minutes pass and she approaches the gas station. She is just a few feet away from it. She fixes her hair and clothes to make a good impression. She breathes in one last time, enters and introduces herself.

— I'm Christine Matias, daughter of Major Quintino. I'm looking for Claudio, the tax collector. Is he home?

— My son went to get a quick bite to eat at a restaurant here close by. I'll send for him. These are my daughters Fabiana and Patricia, and I am Mr. Pereira.

Christine greeted them with kisses on the cheek.

— So you are the famous Christine. I can't believe that I haven't even seen you yet. You stay inside a lot and that's not good. Well, from now on, we can be friends and hang out together. (Fabiana)

— It's a great pleasure to meet you. You, Fabiana and I will be great friends, you can count on it.

— Thank you. I'm also very happy to meet you. I don't go out much because my parents are controlling. They think a major's daughter has to be a bit reserved. They are overprotective.

— Well, that's going to change. Consider yourself part of our gang. We are the craziest kids on the block. (Fabiana)

— Our gang is great. You'll love being a part of it. (Patricia)

— Thanks for inviting me to be part of your group. I think a few relationships and friends won't hurt me.

The conversation continued in a lively manner for some time. Claudio quietly approaches and faces Christine. Their eyes lock and now like magic it seems as if only the two of them exist in the entire universe. The hearts of both hasten upon meeting and an internal heat travels through both bodies.

— My dad called me here. You mean you're the girl who will supervise me? Well, I guess I won't feel so uncomfortable.

The compliment left Christine a little shocked. She never found men so direct.

— My name is Christine; I am the daughter of the major. I'm your new partner at work. Can we begin? I'm looking forward to it.

— Yes, of course. My name is Claudio. We're just in time to start work. The first commercial establishment that we're going to visit today is the butcher shop. It has been three months that the owner hasn't paid taxes and we need to press him for it. I think your presence will help.

— Let's go, then. It was a pleasure to meet you, Fabiana and Patricia. See you later.

The two wave their hands in farewell. Claudio and Christine depart together toward the butcher shop. Christine's thoughts rise intimately and she feels like a fool for having idolized Claudio so much. He was nothing like she'd imagined but he had stirred something inside of her. The feeling that she had to get to know him was like nothing she'd ever experienced. What was it? She couldn't define it, but it was something strong and lasting. The two walk side by side and Claudio tries to start up a conversation.

— Christine, tell me a little about yourself. You are from Recife, right?

— No. I lived in Recife for ten years. Actually, I'm from Alagoas. My childhood was pretty much entirely spent there.

— Have you ever had a boyfriend?

— I had one but it was some time ago. I was going to be a nun. I spent three years of my life in a cloistered convent trying to find a meaning to my life. When I realized I had no vocation I left and I went back to my parents' house.

— It would be a great waste if you were a nun, with all due respect. Nothing against religion but the giving of one's self to God requires too much from a person.

— Well, that's all in the past. I have to focus on my new life and my duties.

The talk suddenly stops and the two continue to walk. The coming and going of people is constant in the downtown area. Mimoso had turned into a regional trade center after the implantation of the railroad. People came from all over the region to visit and shop in its shops. The butcher shop is nearby and Christine can barely contain herself. She didn't know how to act. After all, she was the daughter of the major and had to set an example. The job of tax collector would expose her a lot. Finally, they arrive and Claudio addresses Mr. Helio, the owner of the shop.

— Mr. Helio, we've come here to collect from you the three months of taxes that you owe. The city needs your contribution to invest in education, health and sanitation. Do your duty as a citizen.

— Haven't I told you I'm broke? Business here has not been good. I need an extension on paying you.

— I won't accept any more excuses and if you don't pay, you'll have problems. See this girl with me? She is the major's daughter. He is not satisfied with your defaults. The best thing to do, Sir, would be to pay your debts.

Helio thought for a moment about what to do. At a glance, he looks at Christine and convinces himself that she is the daughter of the major. He opens a drawer, takes out a wad of money and pays. Both thank him and withdraw from the establishment.

The morning is spent working. The two visit homes and businesses. Some taxpayers refuse to pay claiming lack of capital. Christine begins to admire Claudio for his professionalism and confidence. The morning passes and the day is over. The two say goodbye and that they would return to work together again in fifteen days.

The Picnic

The sun advances on the horizon and heats up even more as it's after noon. Movement decreases, farmers come in from the farm, the washerwomen arrive with their loads that they were washing in the Mimoso River, the civil servants are released, the lace-makers get a break at work and everyone can have lunch. Christine is no different from the others and also comes back home at this time. She arrives, opens the door and heads to the main kitchen. Her parents are already present and Gerusa is serving lunch.

— Pardon us for not waiting for you to serve lunch, my daughter, but I arrived tired and hungry because I was in a business meeting. Changing the subject, how was your first day of work? (Major)

— No need to apologize. My first day of work was long and tiring. Claudio and I struggled to convince the taxpayers to pay. However, some have become firm in their positions. Overall, it was a good day's work because I learned a lot. I'm just not sure I want to do this for the rest of my life.

— Tell Claudio that I want the details of those who did not pay. I am the major and I will not tolerate any more delays.

— Did you meet anyone, daughter? Make friends? (Helena)

— Yes, a few people. Claudio's sisters are quite nice.

Gerusa serves Christine and she begins to eat. She remained quiet during this time because she was brought up that way. Gerusa retired from the kitchen and headed to her quarters outside of the house. The three heads of the household remained, having their meals. Christine finishes her lunch, gets up from the table and says goodbye to her parents with kisses on their cheeks. She heads to the balcony of the house where it's well ventilated and cool so she can knit. She picks up her threads and starts knitting. The movement of her agile hands takes her to mysterious worlds where only the imagination can reach. She sees herself dating a man with strong, muscular shoulders, and a firm stance. She imagines her engagement and subsequent marriage. At that moment, an interior anguish punishes and distresses her. The moment passes and she sees herself as the mother of three beautiful children. In her imagination, time passes quickly and she sees herself as a grandmother and a great-grandmother. Death comes and she sees herself in paradise surrounded by angels and by our Lord, Jesus Christ. Her agile hands work and, for a moment, she acknowledges in the cloth that is she is knitting a familiar man's face. She shakes her head and the illusion passes. What was happening to her? Was she crazy, or even possibly in love? She didn't want to believe in this possibility. She keeps working until she hears her name pronounced with incredible intensity. She goes back to the entrance to the garden of her house from where she had heard the voice. She recognizes Fabiana, Patricia and Claudio accompanied by some other young people.

— May we come in, Christine?

— Yes, you may. Make yourselves at home.

There were exactly six young people who entered the garden of the house. They went up the stepladders that gave access to the balcony and met with Christine. Fabiana took care to make introductions of the unknown friends.

— This is my cousin Rafael and these are my friends Talita and Marcela.

Christine greeted them with kisses on the cheek.

— Nice to meet you. If you are Fabiana's friends then you are also friends of mine.

— The pleasure is all mine. Claudio spoke highly of you. (Rafael)

— Well, Christine, we came here to invite you on a nice walk to the top of the Ororubá Mountain. We're going to have a picnic outdoors. Contact with nature is essential for humans to evolve and free themselves from their karma. (Claudio)

— Would you like to go, Christine? You are inside a lot and that's not good. (Fabiana)

— We insist. (They all repeat)

— OK. I'll go. You have convinced me. Wait just a minute I'm going to tell my parents.

Christine enters the house for a moment but is soon back. She meets back up with the group and together they agree to make the trip to the mysterious mountain of Ororubá, the sacred mountain. The seven begin to walk. Christine watches Claudio and concludes that he is the typical rural man: Strong, confident and full of charm. The first day they worked together made a good impression but she still didn't know how she felt about him. She just knew it was a strong and lasting feeling. Well, the picnic was a chance to get to know him better, she thinks. The seven speed up and soon are at the foot of the mountain. Claudio, the leader of the group, stops and asks for everyone to do the same.

— It is important that we hydrate ourselves now so that we don't have problems later. The walk is long and exhaustive. (Claudio)

— I heard that this mountain is sacred and has magical properties. (Talita)

— It's true. Legend has it that a mysterious shaman gave his own life to save his people. From then on the mountain of Ororubá became sacred. They also say that a spirit ancestor named the guardian of the mountain guards all of its secrets. (Fabiana)

— That is not all. At its top is a majestic cave said to be able to fulfill any desire. Dreamers from all over the world seek it to obtain its miracles. However, as far as we know, no one has survived it. (Patricia)

— These stories make me nervous. Wouldn't it be better if we went back? (Christine)

— Don't worry, Christine. -They are just stories. Even if it were true, I would be here to protect you. (Claudio)

— Claudio is not the only one. I'm also a man and I'm willing to help you if you need it. (Rafael)

— What about me? No one's protecting me? I am also a damsel in distress. I'm hurt. (Marcela)

Rafael approaches Marcela and gives her a hug as a sign that she has nothing to fear. All drink water and start the walk. Christine advances a little further and puts herself next to Claudio, in front. She felt unsafe after hearing the information about the mountain. She thinks about the mountain, the guardian and the cave. Intimately she sees herself entering the cave and realizing her greatest wish at that moment. She was also a dreamer like so many who had lost their lives in the cave in search of their dreams. Well, it was necessary to keep her feet on the ground, in harsh reality she was the daughter of the major and this restricted her freedom of action quite a bit in relation to friends, loves and desires. Comparatively, she felt freer in the convent than now. Claudio gives a hand to Christine to help her on the way up because he can see she's struggling. Christine's mind races and she thinks it would be good to have a friend that would support and be loyal and honest to her, a friend such as Claudio. She shakes her head and tries to deviate from the thought. It was impossible because her father would not allow this kind of union. He was a simple tax collector and she was the daughter of a major. They lived in completely different worlds. The group stops once again in order to refresh themselves again. The heat is strong and there is little wind. They were halfway there.

— From here it is possible to see a good part of Mimoso. Do you see, Christine? There's your house. (Claudio)

— The view from here is really privileged. I think the top is even more stunning. The sierra of Mimoso doesn't even look big from this view. (Christine)

— I think it best we keep going. It makes no sense to stay up here for a long time. (Fabiana)

— I also agree. This way we can take longer at the top which is the most important part of the mountain. (Rafael)

Most agree on continuing the walk. After all it was past 1:00 PM Christine already felt a bit tired. Climbing a mountain is extremely exhausting for anyone who's not used to doing so. She remembers the constant challenges that she was submitted to at the convent but none of it was similar to ascending a mountain that everybody had said was sacred. She gathers strength in the depths of her soul and tries very hard so that no one notices her difficulty. Claudio smiles at her and that fills her with strength because for him she would surpass any obstacle. Love, this strange power, has linked the two even without any physical contact. For him, if she had the chance, she would face the guardian and enter the cave to realize her dream of joining him throughout the time they had to be together in life. Even if it cost her her life. After all, what meaning does life have if we're not with those who we really love? An empty life is similar to no life at all. The group advances further and approaches the top. Claudio tries to disguise it but he is fully attracted by the beauty and grace of Christine. From the moment they met something changed in his very being. He couldn't eat right or even do anything without thinking about her. He thinks about how conducive her family's move from Pesqueira to the thriving village of Mimoso was. He thinks about how destiny was generous to have reunited the two practically in the same job. The picnic would be a great opportunity to maybe woo the girl. He had hopes of being accepted in spite of the disparities between them. The difficulties, mainly her prejudiced parents, were obstacles that could be overcome. Eventually the group reaches the top and all celebrate. Now all that was left was to find a good place to picnic. The members of the group divide up into three smaller groups to find the most appropriate place. A few minutes go by and one of the groups gives a signal, whistling. The place was chosen. The whole group gathers again and the picnic is set up. Each member of the group contributed with something for the banquet.

— Do you feel it, Christine? The singing of the birds, the light whisper of the wind, the rural atmosphere, the buzz of insects, all this leads us to places and planes never before visited. Every time I come here I feel like an important part of nature and not like I own it, as some think. (Claudio)

— It's very pretty. Here, in nature, I feel like an ordinary human being and not the daughter of a major and you can't imagine how good this feels. (Christine)

— Enjoy it, Christine. It's not every day you can do that. Prejudice, fear, shame, all this disrupts our day-to-day. Here we can forget that, at least for a moment. (Fabiana)

— In this wild green yonder we can feel, see and fully understand the universe. This miracle happens because the mountain is sacred and has magical properties. (Talita)

— I also want to state my opinion. We are seven young people who seek what? I will answer myself. We seek adventures, new experiences, friendships and even love. However, this is only possible if we are at peace with ourselves, with others and with the universe. It is this longed-for peace we've found here. (Rafael)

— Here everything is a learning experience. The rhythm of nature, the company of you all and this fresh air are lessons that we should take with us for our children and grandchildren. (Marcela)

— This is all a great communion for me. A communion of spirits that leads us to transcend many stages of our lives. (Patricia)

After all give their opinion about what they were feeling in that magical moment they start to serve themselves. The cozy environment made them remain silent throughout the meal. After all finished lunch, Claudio announced:

— Actually, Christine, we didn't come just to have a simple picnic. We are going to set up camp and spend the night here.

Christine, for a moment, changed color and everyone laughed. She was the only one in the group who didn't know.

— Huh? And what about the dangers of the mountain? My dad will kill me if I spend the night here. I think I'm going to go.

— I advise you not to go. The guardian must be lurking, waiting for the best chance to attack. (Fabiana)

— Don't worry, Christine. Didn't I say that I would protect you? As for your father, don't worry, he knows that we will spend the night here. (Claudio)

Christine calms down. It would be better if she stayed with the group because she didn't know the mountain and its mysteries. It would really be scary out there all alone. Who knows what could happen? It was better not to risk it. The afternoon progresses and all collaborate in pitching two tents. They are ready in no time. Claudio and Rafael go out to look for wood to light a fire, with the aim of chasing away wild animals that inhabited the region. The women are alone in the camp, clearing the ground around the tents.

— It's great to come here, Christine. In the evening, this whole place is even more beautiful. After dinner, you will see: It's a total blast. Tell me, is this not better than staying at home? (Fabiana)

— I'm also enjoying it but you should have let me know that you were going to camp here. I was quite surprised. (Christine)

— Have you noticed how Claudio looks at her and vice versa? I think the two of them are in love.(Talita)

— Your eyes are playing tricks on you, Talita. There's nothing between Claudio and I. (Chistine)

— I, for one part, would be very happy to be your sister-in-law. (Patricia)

— I am with you on that. (Fabiana)

— Thanks, you guys. But unfortunately, it is impossible. (Christine)

Christine, for a moment, looked serious and they stopped with the innuendos. Claudio and Rafael return with all the wood necessary to keep the campfire lit all night. Claudio looks at Christine and she seems to correspond. The afternoon progresses and it gets dark. The bonfire lights the surroundings as the night descends. All gather around it and dinner is served by Fabiana and Patricia. Everyone is eating and talking a bit. Claudio moves away from the group and when he gets a certain distance he makes a motion for Christine to accompany him. She catches the signal and also moves away from the group.

— What are we going to do, Christine? You and me, together, contemplating these stars. They appear to be witnesses of what we're both feeling. I think that not only they, but the entire universe feels it.

— You know that's impossible. My parents wouldn't allow it. They're very biased.

— Impossible? You say that to me, here in this sacred mountain? Here nothing is impossible.

— But, but.........

— Don't say another word. Let your heart scream aloud, like mine.

Claudio stepped forward a bit and embraced Christine. Gently, he curved his hand a little bit around her face and patiently touched Christine's lips with his own. The kiss stirred Christine and for a moment, she felt like she was walking on air. A multitude of thoughts penetrated her mind and disturbed her kiss. When it ends, she pulls away and says:

— I'm not ready yet. Forgive me, Claudio.

Christine runs away and goes back to the group. Claudio goes with her. The bonfire crackles and all gather around it because the cold is intense. Rafael is standing beside the fire, ready to tell horror stories about the mountain.

— There once was a dreamer from a small town called Triumph, in the hinterlands of Pajeú. His name was Eulalio. His dream was to become a bandit and assemble his own gang to commit crimes, amass riches, have social power and ostentation and with this also fascinate and seduce many women. However, he did not have the courage and determination needed to do this. He could barely wield a sword. In his land, he had heard of the sacred mountain of Ororubá and its miraculous cave, able to fulfill any desire. Upon hearing this, he did not think twice and packed up to make the coveted trip. He arrived on the mountain, met the guardian, finished the challenges and finally entered the cave. However, his heart was not fully pure and his desires were not righteous. The cave did not forgive him and destroyed his life and his dreams. From then on, his soul began to wander in pain on the mountain. They say he was seen once by hunters exactly at midnight. He was dressed as a bandit and carried a big gun which fired ghost bullets.

— You mean he became brave after he died? Then the cave, in part, carried out his dream. (Talita)

— Not quite, Talita. The cave destroyed the dreamer's life and instead left only his soul with the objects of his desire. Moreover, he is a lost soul stranded in suffering. (Fabiana)

— This is just a story. There are countless dreamers who tried their luck in the cave and so far none of them managed to survive. For this reason it is called the cave of despair. (Rafael)

— I wouldn't go in that cave for anything. My dreams I'll make happen with planning, persistence, dedication and faith. (Marcela)

— I'd go for love. After all, you can't live without taking risks. (Christine)

— Always the romantic. Christine is in love, people. (Patricia)

Everybody laughs except Claudio. He was still resentful and hurt because in a way he had been rejected by Christine. He had opened his heart and his feelings; however, it was not enough to convince her of his love. She had spoken of prejudice from her parents but she had been the prejudiced one. The anguish he felt at the bottom of his chest made him travel back in time to remember an episode that had happened two years ago when he lived in Pesqueira and was dating a beautiful blond, the daughter of the mayor. They dated hidden for three months because she was afraid of the reaction of her parents. One day, the father found out and was not pleased. He hired two lackeys to whip and slap him around. It was a beating he would never forget. That was how he felt now: Slapped, whipped and not by her parents, but by her and her own prejudices. However, he would not give up so easily from life and his own happiness. He would show Christine his value and she would understand how much had been foolish to lose precious time.

Night falls and all are preparing to sleep in their tents. The fire is kept lit to protect them from the vicious animals of the mountain. However, howls can be heard from a certain distance. Christine stirs from one side to the other trying to control her fear. It was the first time she had slept in a sacred place. The hard ground bothered her even more than she thought it would. The howling continues and at that given moment the noise of footsteps is also heard. Christine holds her breath in despair. Could it be the bandit ghost? Or maybe a wild beast ready to devour her? The sounds of footsteps are coming in her direction. A strong wind hits the tent and a mysterious hand appears in the door flap. She is ready to scream but the man who appears says:

— Relax, it's me.

Christine calms down and recuperates from the scare. She recognizes the voice. It was Claudio. But what he was doing in her tent at such an hour? Her countenance, overshadowed by the darkness of night, reflected this doubt. Claudio crouches down and asks:

— I came by to ask you if you've made your wish.

— Wish? What wish?

— The mountain is sacred and at midnight it will grant a desire to hearts in love. I've done mine and you know what? I asked the mountain to bring us together in love forever.

— Do you believe in this? I don't think any mountain will change my father's plans.

— I already told you, the mountain is sacred. Believe me. It can make our dream come true.

That said, Claudio joined hands with Christine and both closed their eyes. Right then, the two hearts plunged into a parallel plane where they were both happy and free. Christine saw herself married to him and as the mother of at least seven children. The moment was enough for them to feel as one, connected with the universe. The current was broken; Claudio said goodbye and Christine tried to fall asleep on the hard, dry floor.

The Descent from the Mountain

As the new day dawns, Claudio rises and begins to wake up the others. Christine is the last to rise. Claudio and Rafael delve into the woods to catch some fish in a pond nearby. It would be their breakfast. Meanwhile, the women try to light the fire with the rest of the leftover wood. Fabiana breaks the silence.

— Sleep well, Christine?

— Not very well. This hard, dry ground hurt my back. It still hurts. (Christine)

— That's the scout's life for you. Get ready because we still have many adventures. (Talita)

— Did you like the walk, in general? (Patricia)

— Yes, I liked it. The mountain breathes an air of tranquility and peace. I loved the contact with nature and your company. (Christine)

— We also enjoyed it, even though this is not our first time. Now you're part of our team. (Patricia)

— Did you settle things with Claudio last night? (Talita)

— We decided not to start a relationship because we live in completely different worlds. (Christine)

— In time, you'll work it out. Love is stronger than the differences and as I said I would be happy to be your sister-in-law. (Fabiana)

— Me too. (Patricia)

— I envy you. Claudio is so cute. Too bad he isn't interested in me. (Talita)

The conversation continued lively among the women but Christine preferred not to be a part of it. Talking about her love, Claudio, hurt her soul because it felt like it would be an impossible love. She knew her parents well and knew they would be totally against this kind of relationship. Her mother still cradled hopes that she would go back to the convent and her father wanted to see her married to a husband of their social level. Both options excluded Claudio from her life but at the same time her heart longed for him; she wanted only him. These were her two “opposing forces” that she would have to reconcile, or even choose between. These “opposing forces” invaded her heart and still left her in doubt. About thirty minutes after they left, Claudio and Rafael come back with a decent amount of fish. The fire was already lit and the fish are placed on the grill. The fish are completely baked and distributed among the members of the group. Claudio says:

— We were fishing and suddenly an old lady appears asking for some fish for her meal. I gave them to her and in thanks she blessed me and said I was going to be very happy. I didn’t know that lady. I’ve never seen her around these parts. She had this look in her eye that intrigued me as if she knew the future.

— May be she’s the guardian? Doesn’t the legend say that she lives here on the mountain? (Fabiana)

— Could be. That’s what I thought when I saw her. (Rafael)

— Then you are very lucky, my brother. There are few people who can achieve happiness. (Patricia)

— She was really weird. I felt a chill when I gave the fish to her. (Claudio)

— I’m practical. I even believe the mountain to be sacred by the experiences I have lived here. But then to believe in guardians and in caves who perform miracles is a lot of ground to cover. Soon, you’re going to try and convince me that there are ghosts and goblins. (Talita)

— If I were you, I wouldn’t doubt it. Claudio is a serious man and is not a liar. (Marcela)

— I also believe him. At the convent they taught me to judge people by their eyes and Claudio was totally sincere when talking about the guardian. He is really privileged to have met her. (Christine)

Silence reigned in those following moments around the camp and the members of the group finished eating their fish. Claudio and Rafael broke down the tents and the women gathered together the objects that they had brought. The group met in prayer thankful for the moments lived in the mountains and began the walk back to the village where they lived. Claudio gently offered his hand to Christine and she accepted. The descent from the mountain was dangerous for beginners. Physical contact with Claudio made Christine's heart jump even more. This man was making her so crazy that she almost forgot social conventions when she was with him up on the mountain. They were moments that had the power to take her to parallel planes where no one could reach her. She had felt really happy in these moments. However, on the way down the mountain, she would have to abandon her dreams of fantasy and face the harsh reality. A reality where she was the daughter of a corrupt, authoritarian and adamant major. Aside from that, she lived for the moments when Claudio held her and kissed her. Christine squeezes Claudio's hand with force to make sure he's really present there, by her side. She had already lost her grandparents and wouldn't be able to take another loss. The group descends from the top and has already gone half of the distance down the steep mountain paths. Claudio, the leader of the group, stops and asks for everyone to do the same. All drink water and continue walking. Christine thinks about her mother and the scolding that she would receive because she had spent the entire day away from home. She treated her like a child, unable to choose her own path. By her influence, she had entered a convent and spent three years of her life as a recluse. She was only allowed out on accompanied walks and only with the permission of the Mother Superior. In that time, she would learn Latin and the foundations of the Christian religion. Culture and knowledge were the only positive things to come out of her stay there. Mostly, it was a wasted part of her life because she had no desire to be a nun. She was tired of being the good girl and obedient as this only brought her losses. The "opposing forces" that she carried within had to be resolved. The group accelerates its pace and in a short time they travel all the way back home. They say goodbye to each other and all return to their homes.

The Major's Abuses

Christine's reception went smoothly. Neither of her parents complained that she spent the night on the sacred mountain. After all, she had not been alone. After talking with her parents she took a bath, adjourning to her room, and fell sleep as she felt exhausted. The major and his wife are in the living room, talking. A clapping noise can be heard and Gerusa promptly goes to the door to open it. Lenice, a farmer, waits to be attended.

— How may I help you?

— I want to talk to the major. It is very important.

— Come in. He is in the living room.

Lenice enters and goes to the living room.

— Mr. Major, I wanted to talk to you, Sir. It's about my newborn son, Jose.

— What about him? The father doesn't want to take responsibility? Do you need help to raise him?

— No, nothing of the sort. I wish that you, Sir, would be the Godfather of his baptism.

— What? Godfather? To which important family do you belong?

— I'm a Silva and we work in agriculture.

— It's impossible. I wouldn't be the friend of a simple member of the Silva family even if I were the last man on Earth. You should check yourself before you come here with such requests.

— Mr. Major you have no heart.

The poor woman, in tears, removes herself from the room and leaves. She dreamed of being a friend of the major's just like many from the village did. Her son would have many more chances to grow if he were the major's godson. He would have access to education, health care and a dignified job because everything in that village depended on the influence of the major. All, without exception, wanted some kind of connection with him to have these privileges. Those who could not were relegated to a world of misery and suffering.

After driving out the farmer, the major prepares to go to the police station. His wife, Helena, straightens her clothes.

— Did you see that, woman? What impertinence! A major of my worth cannot be the friend of a simple Silva.

— These people here are dying to be your friends. Gold diggers!

— If they were at least traders, I'd take it. Have you ever seen anything like it? A major, friends with farmers.

— I'm glad you put her in her place. I don't think that any more farmers will dare to come here.

The major says goodbye to his wife with a kiss. He starts walking, opens the door and leaves. He concentrates on what he's about to do. Ever since he had been sworn in officially by the mayor as the main political authority in the region, he had not yet taken any active decisions. The figure of the "nice" major was already annoying him. He had to step up to be respected by other authorities. The major and the colonel had key roles in the consolidation of an unfair structure called the 'group of Colonels,' which reigned at the time. From this unjust structure they reveled in power and pageantry. The major keeps walking and soon he is already approaching the station. He is fully convinced in what he is about to do. He learned, in his tragic childhood in Maceió, how to make decisions in the timeliest manner and he recognized that now was the best time. He picks up the pace to avoid regrets and guilt. He arrives at the police station, opens the front door and announces:

— Delegate Pompeu, we have an important matter to discuss.

The major delivers a list to the delegate in his chamber.

— What's this?

— This is the complete list of all delinquent taxpayers. I will not tolerate any more delays and I demand that you, sir, as delegate, will handle this.

— Did you give them an extension on paying?

— Yes, I did everything in my power. The tax collector, Claudio, told me that they give lame excuses in order not to pay.

— I don't see what I can do. The law does not allow me to take any action.

— I must remind you, Mr. Pompeu, that your dear post of delegate will be at risk if you do not take any further action. The law I know serves the strongest and as major I tell you to immediately imprison all these scoundrels and don't release them until they pay their debts.

Delegate Pompeu shook his head and called his two officers to start arresting the victims. The major is satisfied because his demands are being met. This would be the first of many arbitrary acts that he would take as the greatest political authority figure in the region.

Mass

It was a beautiful Sunday morning. The chapel bells chimed announcing the Sunday mass. In the vestry, Father Chiavaretto is preparing for another celebration. Chiavaretto was the official priest of Mimoso. Originally from Venice, Italy, the son of a middle-class family, he had been ordained in 1890. His priestly activity started in his native land in the same year of his ordination and lasted until 1908. This year, by determination of the Bishop of Venice he was officially transferred to Brazil. His mission was to spread the Gospel and to catechize those who still persisted in paganism. In two years of hard work he had achieved progress in the small village. However, one of the goals to be achieved was to get greater numbers at mass. In the beginning, when he arrived in the village, the presence of the population at mass was larger. Over time, people lost enthusiasm simply because the mass carried out by Chiavaretto was entirely in Latin. It was an official determination of the Church at that time.

Before starting the celebration, the priest takes a brief moment of reflection. The time in Venice came to his mind and he remembered the fate of each of his brothers and sisters. One of them decided to be a soldier in the army and left to create an integrated front of peace in other country. He had always had a tendency to protect the other children. One sister left to become a nun and another married and had four children. The two followed opposite paths in their lives but neither forgot the other or stopped being friends. Both lived in Venice, Italy. He became a priest but not by choice but by a sign of fate. He was called by Jesus. The happenings that made him decide to become a priest were as follows: When he was a child, he was playing quietly with one of his friends on a bridge that sits exactly over a river. The game they were playing was tag. Excited over the game, he climbed through the railing of the bridge to get away from his opponent. His legs trembled, he got dizzy and taking a false step he fell exactly into the river. The current was strong as the river was fully flooded. Chiavaretto tried to swim but he had no experience in the water. Gradually he was sinking and his friend just watched because he didn't know how to swim either. At that moment there were no adults around. Little by little, Chiavaretto was losing strength and also consciousness. When he felt he was near his end, he called out the holy name of Jesus. Quickly, he felt a powerful hand holding him and a voice saying:

— Pedro, fear not!

That was his name: Pedro Chiavaretto. The mighty hand lifted him up and out of the water. When he was saved, at the river bank, the mysterious man disappeared. From that day on, Pedro Chiavaretto devoted himself solely to religion and became a priest. This experience was his secret, he didn't tell anyone.

The brief moment of reflection passes and the priest heads to the altar. He looks at the congregation and verifies that it is the same exact lineup of people as always: The rich and powerful, sitting in the best pews and the less fortunate in the others. This type of division distressed him because it was exactly the opposite of what he learned at the seminary. People are equal before God and have the same importance. What distinguishes human beings and makes them special are their talents, charisma and other qualities. Even so, he could not do anything. With the proclamation of the Republic and the Constitution of 1891 there was an official separation of church and state. Brazil became, from that moment on, a constituent country with no official religion. The church lost much of its power and privileges too. With that, the Group of Colonels (reigning in the northeast) were supreme in their decisions, decisions that the church couldn't go against.

The priest starts the celebration and the only ones who really pay attention to his words are the devout Christine and Helena, as both know Latin. The others went to church just to look at the clothes and styles of the others and to gossip. They had no idea of the true meaning of mass. The priest speaks about forgiveness and about the fact that we must be attentive to the signs coming from our hearts. He says that this is the best compass for lost travelers. The mass continues and reaches the moment of communion. When the priest turns bread and wine into the body and blood of Jesus Christ, Christine seems to see Claudio at that altar, next to the Father. She shakes her head and the vision disappears. It was the second time that something like this happened to her. The first time it happened she was knitting on the porch of her home. What was happening to her? Her thoughts wouldn't even respect mass. Christine resolves not to take communion because she wasn't prepared and did not feel totally pure to take part in it. Helen does. The celebration continues and Christine tries to focus on the priest's sermon. She pays attention to every word uttered by him. At that moment, finally she is able to forget Claudio a little and forget the wonderful picnic. She almost gave herself to him on the mountain. A fear of judgment and of her father held her back. The priest gives the final benediction and Christine feels more alleviated. She wouldn't have to worry about holding back her thoughts anymore.

Reflections

Christine, along with her parents, abandon the dependencies of the small chapel of St. Sebastian. The major says goodbye to them and goes to take care of business in the building of the Residents Association. The two return home. Along the way, Christine begins to reflect on the sermon heard just a moment ago from the priest. Had she received forgiveness from her mother after leaving the convent? Had she been forgiven? The answer to both questions is no. Her mother, disappointed after her exit from the convent, was never again the same mother who she had learned to love and respect. She was no longer loving or showed her any kind of caring emotion as before. Her mother was no longer her friend, only a companion. Time and again, she spoke of the convent and commented how she would be so happy if she had a daughter who was a nun. She still fed her own hopes that Christine would go back there. As for her own fate, Christine still harbored doubts. She was sure about the feelings he had for Claudio but was afraid to surrender totally to this passion and end up hurt.

Christine had learned, at the convent, that men had many sides to them and could not be trusted. As for the fact of following her heart, she had refused to listen to it in the most crucial moments of her life. She didn't listen when it said not to get involved with the son of the gardener in the convent. Once expelled, he abandoned her without explanation. She also didn't listen to it when it asked her to give in to Claudio, on the mountain. Instead, she preferred to obey social conventions and fear. Both times she refused to listen to her heart, she was hindered. Christine makes a pact with herself and accepts to listen to it on the next opportunity. Father Chiavaretto's mass had proven helpful.

Sucavão

It was a calm Tuesday morning. The day before, a torrential rain had filled the rivers and streams. The place was bustling with many bathers from all over the region having fun in the Mimoso River. Meanwhile, the group of young friends, headed by Claudio was on their way to Christine's residence. They would ask her to go on another special trip. They arrive at the residence and clap their hands to be heard. Gerusa, the maid of the house, answers the door.

— What do you want?

— We're here to talk to Christine. Is she home?

— She is. Wait a moment. I'll call her.

A few moments later, Christine appears smiling and ready to talk to them.

— Gerusa told me that you guys wanted to talk to me. What about?

Claudio, the leader of the group, spoke up.

— We're here to invite you to go on an interesting trip with us. With yesterday's rain, the rivers and streams of the region overflowed. The entire town is enjoying it. At the Frexeira Velha farm, near here, there is a very special place we want to show you. What do you say?

— If you promise there won't be any surprises like there was that time at the picnic, I'll go. (Christine)

— There won't be. You will be delighted with the place. (Fabiana)

— We promise to show you a very special morning. (Rafael)

The other members of the group also encourage Christine to accept and she ends up agreeing. After all, she wasn't doing anything important at that moment. Going out a little would help her to better reflect on some ideas. With Christine's consent, the group started walking towards a destination that she ignored. Claudio offered her his arm and she accepted, following the instincts of her heart. She had learned this from the priest. Physical contact made Christine dive into parallel universes far beyond the imagination of an ordinary human being. In these places, there was no space for anyone except for her and her beloved. She was married with at least seven children, all from Claudio. Her prejudiced and morally unstable parents lacked the power to affect her in her own imagination. If the mountain of Ororubá were really sacred, it would proceed with their request and make these plans a reality. Although this was almost impossible for two reasons. First, because she was the daughter of a mother who still harbored hopes of her becoming a nun. Second, she had a father who projected a future for her (in his opinion a happy one), by marrying her to someone from her own social level. In addition, both were extremely prejudiced.

The group stops a little so that everyone can rehydrate. Claudio wouldn't let go of Christine's arm for a moment. In his mind, Christine would only be his, seeing as how they were interlinked. From the moment he met her, his life changed. He began to give less importance to drinking and smoking. He practically stopped doing so. His friends also noticed changes. He had become a more charismatic and cheerful man. He did not complain anymore about work or bills. He became illuminated by God's love. For Christine, he was willing to do anything: To face the dreaded Major and his wife; to face public opinion; to face God and the world if necessary. He was getting to know true love, unlike other times he had dated.

The group accelerates their pace and in about ten minutes they reach the Frexeira Velha farm. They turn to the right and walk a few more feet as a shortcut took them to the brink of a railroad. They finally arrive at their destination and Christine is amazed. It faces a natural pool carved in stone and that is overlooking a small stream.

— So this is what you wanted to show me. It is sensational!

— We knew you'd like it. It is a great place to relax a little. It's called Sucavão. (Claudio)

They all run to this small wonder of nature. Claudio moves away a little from Christine and starts to jump around crazily in the water. He dives and stays submerged for a few seconds. Christine gets worried and starts looking for him throughout the pool. When she least expects it, two strong arms hold her thighs and Claudio resurfaces, hugging her.

— Were you looking for me?

Christine doesn't say anything and rests her little arms on Claudio's shoulders. He feels the moment and moves closer to her. His insistent lips look for hers. The two find each other and cause a storm of applause. Christine and Claudio turn towards the others and laugh. Their relationship was confirmed. Everyone continues to enjoy the pool. Claudio and Christine do not move from each other's side. The group spends the whole morning in Sucavão and then later on all return to their homes.

The Market

A very sunny Wednesday morning arises and Christine has just awoken. She gets up out of bed and takes a bath. She enters the bathroom, turns on the faucet and the cold water floods her entire body. At that moment, her mind travels and lands exactly in the events of the previous day. She thinks about Claudio's embrace and the kiss. The initial physical contact made her even more certain about what she felt for him. It was something really enduring. She turns off the water, soaps up and fear begins to take a hold of her intimate thoughts. What would become of them when her parents found out? Would love be stronger than prejudice and social conventions? Had the mountain really answered her request? The answer to these questions she didn't know. The only thing they could do was to both enjoy the moment and hope that it would last forever.

She turns the water back on and the previous fear disappears. She was willing to fight for this love even if it cost her dearly. The water from the faucet makes her remember Sucavão and how that place was magical. She thinks everyone should be like the flowing river which gives itself completely to its destiny. That's how she would act in relation to her love, Claudio. The cold water starts to bother her and she decides to turn it off. She takes two towels and begins to dry off. After completely drying herself, she dresses and goes to the kitchen to have breakfast. Upon arriving, she finds Gerusa serving her parents.

— Up already? You look great. What happened?

— Nothing, Mother. I just had a good night.

— My daughter is a good girl, woman. She wouldn't do anything against our principles. (Major)

An icy chill toured Christine's body and at that moment it seemed her parents had guessed her thoughts. She decides to keep quiet so as not to arouse suspicion.

— What do you say we go to the fair today? I need fruit, vegetables and beans. (Helena)

— I'll gladly go with you, mom.(Christine)

— Well, I can't. I'm going to take care of business. (Major)

The two finish up breakfast and go to the market. The Mimoso market had become a big event that lured visitors from all over the region. On that day, it was intensely busy and trade flourished. Christine and Helena approach Olivia's fruit stand and at that moment the heavens seemed to cross in the exchange of glances between Christine and Claudio.

— You around here? I wasn't expecting that. (Christine)

— My mother left me in charge of her tent. What wouldn't a child do for his mother? How are you, miss?

— Very well.

— I didn't know you two were such good friends.

Christine disguises her feelings for Claudio a bit and responds:

— He is part of the group of friends who I go out with and besides, he's my coworker, did you forget?

— Oh, yes. The tax collector.

Claudio winks at Christine as a sign of complicity. The two had to fake it until the right time. Claudio asks:

— What will you have?

— I want two dozen bananas, three papaya and six mangoes. (Helena)

Christine pays attention to every masculine detail of her love and is impressed. She had no doubts: He was the man that she wanted, no matter how many obstacles she had to overcome. She had learned, at the convent, that a winner was one who had the courage to dare. Claudio gives them the fruits and Christine and Helena go to another station. The market will be open until 2:00 PM.

The Case of the Cow

Major Quintino, as one of the pioneers of the region, became a rich plantation owner and consequently one of the largest cattle ranchers in the region. One day, his employees were crossing the cattle over the railroad in order to have access to another part of the ground. By coincidence, that same instant, a train with great speed appeared on the horizon. The employees rushed the crossing and the train conductor tried to stop, but without success. One of the cows was hit by the train and died on impact. The driver continued on his trip and the employees were appalled. They got together and decided to tell all to the major.

When the major heard the story, he ordered his employees to put a giant rock on the tracks of the railroad. In this same time, the major remained perched waiting for the train. It appeared on the horizon right on time and when the engineer noticed the rock he stopped short to try to avoid the crash. Luckily, he was successful and no one was hurt. The driver vexed, got off the train and asked:

— Who put that stone in the middle of the railroad?

At that moment, the major approaches him and inquires:

— What is your name, Sir?

— My name is Roberto. Tell me, who put this stone in my path?

— It was my men who placed it here. I see that today you managed to stop the train. However, just yesterday, sir, you were not successful and hit one of my cows.

— It wasn't my fault. The train came at full speed and when I realized the cow was still there, it was too late.

— Your apologies are of no use to me. Don't worry: I won't denounce you to the authorities or demand you to pay for the cow. However, starting tomorrow, every time that you pass through this village you will be obligated to stop in front of my house ask if anyone of my family will be traveling. If so, you will wait as long as it takes for us to get ready. If not, you can follow along on your journey. Are we clear?

— Well, I guess I have no choice. Fine.

The major orders his employees to withdraw the stone so the train could continue on its journey.

The Press

Major Quintino was famous throughout the region for his methods of torture. The most well-known of them was, without a doubt, the dreaded press. It was an iron instrument with five rings, one for placing on the neck, two for each hand and two for each leg. The major's enemies were whipped in the press, often to the death.

Once, the major had three horses stolen and the thief was seen by one of his employees. The thief disappeared for a time and the major failed to locate him. With the case closed, the thief decided to return and was seen strolling around Mimoso. The major immediately knew it was him and sent his employees to detain him. The thief was caught and placed in the press. Tortured and humiliated, the thief confessed to the crime, and said he sold the horses to get some change. The angered major did not forgive him and ordered his employees to flog him all night long. The thief succumbed to his injuries and died. The major's employees picked up the body and buried him. He was one of the victims of this archaic system of society; A system that kills even before judgment.

Message

It already had been a couple of weeks that Claudio and Christine were dating secretly. The two saw each other every fifteen days at work or in other situations with their group of friends. These meetings were well used by the two who exchanged caresses and kisses when no one was looking. However, this situation was not comfortable to Claudio. He still felt insecure with Christine's resolution of not telling anyone about their relationship. He wanted to vent and tell the whole world how happy and fulfilled he felt. To this end, he called Guilherme (a street kid) and handed him a note addressed to Christine. The boy quickly obeyed.

Guilherme arrives at Christine's house, claps his hands and yells to be heard. Gerusa comes to the door.

— What do you want, boy?

— This note's for Miss Christine. Can you call her, please?

— You can give it to me. I'm trustworthy.

— No. This note is to be delivered by hand.

Reluctantly, Gerusa goes to call Christine. A great curiosity was building in her mind. She was the maid of this family for ten years and in her opinion nothing that happened in that house went unnoticed by her eyes. Since Christine was a child she took care of her and her interests more so than her own mother. She wasn't about to be left out of this. Christine is in her room and when she receives the news she goes promptly to meet the boy. She takes the note and Gerusa accompanies her. Immediately, Christine locks herself in her room leaving behind an anguished Gerusa. She felt unappreciated by Christine's attitude. The years of companionship and complicity went to dust in that moment. After all, what could be so important to the point of Christine wanting to hide it?

Meeting

With her heart racing, Christine begins to read the note written by Claudio. In it, he invites her to a meeting to be held in his home. Christine is doubtful and thinks it might be risky to go there. After all, the evil tongues of the village could raise suspicions about the two of them and that news could end up directly with her parents. She wanted to preserve the relationship. On the other hand, she didn't want to hurt Claudio and provoke an estrangement between them. The feelings she had for her love were more important. She thinks a bit and decides to go. Certainly it was worth risking it for her one true love. The consequences, if any, they would face together.

Christine gets ready and leaves without giving explanation to Gerusa or to anyone else. Her mind wanders to places unknown to any other person who didn't know of their history. She thinks about the convent, the son of the gardener and about her love, Claudio. The convent appears as an old image that she wants to forget. There, she learned Latin, the fundamentals of religion, respect for people and the true meaning of the word love. Still at the convent, she remembers the gardener's son and the importance in maturation that decision had and how it had changed her life. She had given up being a nun and had taken all the consequences of it, such as the disappointment and contempt of her mother. She thinks about Claudio and with that thought a ray of hope fills her entire being. Her hope is that they stay together backed by an eternal love, even if they had to pass insurmountable barriers. The picnic on the mountain comes to her mind and how they were happy although not together. She remembers the hug, kiss and wish that she made on the sacred mountain. In a way, her request had already begun to be answered as her and Claudio were dating. Going to church and learning what she had, had her helped her begin the relationship in Sucavão. That magical place had the power to enchant and bring two hearts together. She had learned to be like the flowing river, delivering herself completely to her destiny, Claudio. It was for him that she decided to go to the encounter.

Christine accelerates her steps, driven by curiosity. She is already just a few feet from the place. She looks around and makes sure that no one is following or watching her. The instinct of self-protection was stronger than anything. After all, every precaution taken was necessary in a relationship that was not yet confirmed. She goes a little further and finally arrives at Claudio's home. She knocks on the door and waits for it to be answered. The door opens and Claudio pulls her inside. To Christine's surprise, Claudio's entire family is reunited.

— Here is my girlfriend, Christine, as I promised. We've been dating for two weeks now. This is my mother, Olivia (he said pointing to a woman with strong features that appeared to be about fifty years old). The others you already know: My sisters Fabiana and Patricia, and my father, Paulo Pereira.

Christine is breathless with this presentation. What was Claudio doing? Hadn't the two agreed to date secretly? Awkwardly, Christine greets everyone. Claudio makes her sit at the table where everyone is.

— Welcome to the family, Christine. My husband and I approve of this relationship. You're a serious and well accomplished girl. (Olivia)

— Thank you. I wasn't expecting this. Claudio took me by surprise. (Christine)

— I couldn't take this situation anymore. My parents had the right to meet the beloved girl of my heart. (Claudio)

That said, Claudio entangled Christine in his arms and kissed her.

— I already told Christine how glad I would be to be her sister-in-law. In addition, I want to say that I admire your determination and grit. (Fabiana)

— Me too. I wish happiness to you both. (Patricia)

Paulo Pereira begins to serve the cocktails and Christine is a bit withdrawn, although happy. The conversation begins to travel to and from various subjects and Christine is the center of attention. Everyone compliments her posture and style. Time passes and Christine doesn't even realize it. After they got to know her a bit, Christine says goodbye and Claudio accompanies her to the door. They hug and kiss each other before saying goodbye. Claudio's attitude showed Christine that his intentions were serious and real.

Confession

It was a beautiful Thursday morning and Christine prepares to go see Father Chiavaretto. She's in a line of five people. Anxiety, nervousness and doubt fill her entire being. The preparations she made before her confession hadn't taken effect. All that she considers to be sins come to her mind: Omissions, errors and a lack of caution. However, she still wasn't sure if she'd even tell the whole truth. On the other hand, if she didn't, she would continue to remain in sin. The nuns of the convent where she stayed for three years were quite strict in that sense. The queue empties and Christine is next. She enters the confessional and kneels.

— Hail Mary, full of grace.

— Conceived without sin.

— Confess your sins, my daughter.

— Well, Father, I have a great secret that weighs on me. It's been a while that I have been dating the tax collector, Claudio. This secret is killing me, father. Sometimes, I can't even sleep at night. However, if I tell, I'm sure my parents will be against this relationship because they are very biased. What do I do, Father? I don't want to break up with Claudio because I love him.

— My daughter, you must tell the whole truth. Only that can set your conscious free of remorse. Talk to your parents and show them your point of view. When love is true it overcomes all obstacles. I think I'm going to give you a penance to reflect better. Pray ten Our Fathers and five Hail Mary's.

Christine thanks the Father and goes to fulfill her penance. She would reflect on the advice given by him.

Gossip

Christine going to Claudio's house did not pass completely unnoticed and neither did the ways that he treated her in public. Beatrice, Claudio's neighbor, was suspicious that this visit was not just a friendly one. After the fact, she decided to investigate the two to see if she was right in her suspicions. She ended up finding out the whole truth. For a time, she remained silent out of fear of the reaction of the major and his wife. Later on, she did not feel that this whole situation was very fair. With a sense of justice, she decided to go to the major's house. She arrives, claps her hands and is met by Gerusa.

— What do you want?

— I want to talk to the major and his wife.

— They are in the living room. Come in.

Quickly, Beatriz comes in and stands before the two.

— Good day, Major Quintino and Madame Helena. I have something serious to talk to you about. Is your daughter home?

— She went to confession. (Helena)

— Even better. I want to speak to you about her. She's secretly dating Claudio, the tax collector. There. I said it. (Beatriz)

— What? Are you crazy, woman? My daughter is a good girl. She wouldn't get involved with a guy like that. (Major)

— I can't believe it either. I still want her to be a nun. (Helena)

— I assure you that what I said is true. I saw the two embraced and kissing with my own eyes, I swear as sure as I stand here.(Beatriz)

— Then she betrayed us. She is mistaken if she thinks she's going to stay with him. I wouldn't mix my name or my blood with a simple Pereira. (Major)

— I can't believe it either. I will not let her get married. (Helena)

— Well, I think I have fulfilled my Good Samaritan's deed. I can't stand to see injustice.(Beatriz)

— Thanks for letting us know. I will make it up to you.

The major stands up and hands over a wad of cash to Beatrice. She leaves happily and quietly out of bungalow thinking that she has fulfilled her mission.

Voyage to Recife

The news that Christine was dating a simple tax collector had not left the major happy. With his pride wounded, he planned an ending to this vexatious situation. He sent a note to the mayor and to the Colonel of Rio Branco inviting them on a trip to Recife. The three would talk to the Governor about business, politics and personal matters. With all settled, the major packed his bags as he was leaving the next day for Recife.

The day started out with the sun hotter than ever. The major arises without delay and goes to take a bath. He enters the bathroom, turns on the faucet and the cold water floods his entire body. The cold water reassures his conscience but his blood is still boiling. He remembers Christine when she was a child. She was as sweet and tender as a flower. Once she was playing with dolls and invited him to play as well. He awkwardly accepted. Christine played the role of mother and he the father doll. They spent a long time simulating conversations and situations within a family. There was a moment she said: -My doll is lucky to have a father like you. It moved him quite a bit and he had to withdraw from playing so that she didn't see him crying. What had happened to that little sensitive girl? How had she been able to betray him like that? When she was born, he did not deny having a certain unfavorable feeling for her having been born female. The most suitable for him was to have had a son, someone to succeed him in tyranny, political power and social ostentation. But over time, she showed her value and won over everyone in the family. His plans changed to arranging a good son-in-law to take care of his daughter and succeed him. These plans seemed to be going downhill as of the latest news he had received. Quickly, the major turns off the water and leaves the bathroom. He was in a hurry to put his plan into action.

He goes to the kitchen and has breakfast. He greets his wife but pretends to not see his daughter. Christine takes the initiative and talks to him, but he responds bitterly and dryly to her. She thinks her father's attitude is strange, but remains silent. The major has his breakfast, lets them know he will be gone a few days, gets up and leaves. Already out of the house, he begins to form a plan of action: First he would go to the police station and second board the train bound for Recife. His plans translate into the state the major is in, restless, uneasy and disappointed. He was uneasy about finding himself in this current situation: The father-in-law of a simple civil servant. He felt apprehensive in not knowing exactly what results he would achieve on this trip. He was disappointed at being betrayed by his only beloved daughter. What else could happen? Well, he didn't know. A few minutes later he can already see the police station and his hatred grows even more. Who did that paltry tax collector think he was? Not even in his wildest dreams could he join the Matias family. This was a family that was traditional and that had conquered virtually all the land west of Pesqueira. Who were the Pereiras? Just a simple merchant family who were not up to his daughter's level. He wouldn't allow the two stay together as long as he lived.

Finally, the major enters the station and goes to the office of Delegate Pompeu. He nods his head and begins to speak.

— Mr. Pompeu, I have a job for you. I want you to arrest a man for me.

— Why? Who's the man?

— It's a man who has disrespected my daughter. His name is Claudio, the tax collector.

— Claudio? He seemed like such a good lad.

— I also thought so. However, he has disappointed me with his attitude. As of today, he's my enemy and must suffer for his betrayal. I want you to arrest him immediately and do not release him until I say so.

— All right, I'll do it. My men will arrest him today.

— That's what I wanted to hear. You are a good friend, Pompeu. Who knows when I'm mayor you might be my secretary.

— At your service, Sir.

The two depart and the major heads in the direction of the railway station. A train bound for Recife would leave in a few minutes. The major's steps become more and more regular and he feels better. The first step of his plan was accomplished. His enemy, in a short time, would be powerless behind bars. Christine would have to get used to living without him. The major begins to design, in his head, the second step of his plan, a step that only he and God knew about. He arrives at the station, buys a ticket, says hello to the staff and boards.

Upon entering the train, he comes across Rio Branco's Colonel (Mr. Henrique Cergueira). He sits beside him and is happy the Colonel has met his request. They start to talk and remember their pioneering days. They remember the resistance of the natives and how they had to be cruel to take possession of their land. They were moments of glory for the two. Major Quintino and Farmer Osmar took possession of the lands in the Mimoso region and Colonel Henrique Cergueira took the land in the Rio Branco region, a village located west of Mimoso. The colonel remembers how he was able to convince a native family that he wouldn't do them any harm. Time passed quickly for the two remembering that not-so-distant past.

The train whistles signaling that it will make a stop. The major and the colonel go out to have a quick snack. They arrive at the bar near the Pesqueira railway station.

— What will you have, gentlemen?

— Two cups of the good stuff you have there and a plate of roast beef. (Major)

— Well, Major, you've asked me to go to Recife but haven't explained to me why we are really going there.

— I have my plans but I can't talk now. I have to resolve an issue with the governor and then have a serious talk with you.

— You can't give me a hint?

— No. Nothing more than what I already said.

The conversation cooled and the two finished up their snack. They left the bar, went back to the train station and boarded the train again because it was about to leave. Upon entering the train, the mayor was already present. The major is glad that he has also answered his request. They remain in the same car to talk about their families, soccer stars and women. Talking about his family, the major cites his wife and daughter as his greatest treasures. The colonel speaks about his son, Bernard, and his daughter Karina and ensures that they will be his legitimate successors as much in politics as in their way of acting. The mayor says that he has no children because his wife is barren but he is happily married anyway. Speaking of sports, they cite Sport Recife and Nautico as the best soccer teams in the state. About women, the major affirms that he loves all kinds. The colonel says he prefers dark-skinned women with slender bodies. The mayor claims that he doesn't look at any other women besides his wife. The others laugh at that statement. They keep talking and the time passes quickly. The train makes several stops before arriving at its final destination, Recife.

The three land and immediately hail a vehicle to take them to the palace which is the seat of the state government. In the car, the driver introduces himself and asks a few questions. They respond continuing in conversation. The driver talks about Recife, highlighting its bridges, beaches, rivers, churches and other landmarks. He concludes by saying that the people of Recife are hospitable and friendly. The major doesn't pay much attention to the conversation as he is focused on his plans. The conversation with the governor would be decisive for him. Sometime later the car stops in front of the palace and all get out.

The three roam the few feet that separate them from the palace and enter by the main gate. Inside they are instructed to the cabinet and told that the governor will see them. They enter the area and are received by the governor. The mayor makes the proper introductions.

— This is Major Quintino, the greatest political authority in the region of the thriving village of Mimoso. And this is the Colonel of Rio Branco (Henrique Cergueira), an important trailblazer of the western region of Pesqueira.

— I've heard talk of Mimoso. This place has become an important trading post of Pernambuco, with the deployment of the railway. As for you, Colonel, you are notorious for your great achievements. It's an honor to welcome you here in this building which represents the strength of our people and the pride of our state. What can I help you with?

— The major should know. He has invited us to come here but has not let us in on the reason why. (Colonel of Rio Branco)

— It's the truth. About the next elections for Mayor of Pesqueira, I would like, with all due respect, Sir, if you would support me for successor of our dear friend, Mr. Horacio Barbosa.

— What? The Pesqueira region has many colonels. One of them should be the successor.

— None of them has my wit and political power. I have implemented an instrument of torture called the press and it has become the absolute terror of my enemies. I'm no longer just a simple major. Mr. Horacio and Mr. Henrique, present here, can testify in my favor.

— It's the truth. The Major Quintino stands out in the city of Pesqueira. He is an important member of our system of "Colonels." I, as Colonel of Rio Branco, show him my unrestricted support.

— I also support him. He was one of the first pioneers of the land in the region of Mimoso. His attitude with the natives was extremely important and decisive. He is the only one who can replace me as mayor.

— Well, if you two approve his candidacy and attest, I don't object. I support him as the next Mayor of Pesqueira.

The three applaud the governor and Major Quintino pulls the Colonel of Rio Branco into another room. They would have a private conversation.

— What do you want to tell me? Why did you pull me in that way?

— I have something to offer to you, Sir. I have a beautiful daughter named Christine and want her to marry as soon as possible.

I thought about possible suitors. Then I remembered your son Bernardo and how he is your rightful successor both in attitude as well as politics. I think he would be a perfect match for my daughter. What do you say? It would be great if the two united our families.

Sir Henrique thinks for a moment and answers.

— I was also thinking about getting Bernardo married. There comes a time when a man has to wise up and lay down roots. Your daughter would be a great advantage for him. However, wasn't she going to be a nun?

— She's already abandoned that idea. My wife filled her head when she was a girl. Now, she's settled and ready to get married. When can we set up the wedding?

— I think a month is enough to take care of the arrangements. We have to have a big party and invite our fellow companions within the system.

— Of course. Everything for the happiness of the two. I cannot wait until my house is full of grandchildren.

The two shake hands and return to the governor's office where they join the mayor. They bid farewell to the highest political authority of the state and head to a nearby hotel. They would spend two more days in the capital of Pernambuco participating in ceremonies and enjoying the beauty of the beaches.

Return to the Inland

The three travelers from the interior depart from the hotel and the facilities of the capital of Pernambuco. They charter a vehicle directly to the train station. In a short time they arrive at their destination. They get out of the car, buy their tickets and finally embark. They sit in the first class section. The mayor and the Colonel of Rio Branco start talking but the major appears thoughtful, his thoughts scattered. The images of Claudio and Christine come to his mind. No, they could never be together because they belonged to entirely different worlds. He didn't raise his daughter to be a clerk at a retail store. She deserved so much more than that because she was the daughter of a major, the highest political authority in the region of Mimoso. In his mind, the major sees Claudio in jail and it gives him a strange feeling of pleasure. Who told him to betray him like that? Who authorized him to dream so high? He was simply paying the price of his own madness. The major envisions the entire scene and has no regrets. After all, he was looking after the interests of his daughter and her future.

The train jolts and the major begins to enter into conversation with his two companions. They talk of their future projects. The Colonel of Rio Branco yearns to make his village a town in a few years and later earn its independence from the city of Pesqueira. He dreams of being mayor and getting good positions for his friends and family. The mayor speaks about leaving politics and becoming a great landlord in the hinterlands, around Vila Bela. He speaks about caring for herds of cattle and planting extensive plantations. The money he got by fraudulent measures would be enough to accomplish this plan. The major is more modest. He wants to see his daughter married and with children. He also is counting on the word of the governor who promised to support him for mayor. The three continue to talk and an employee offers them juice and snacks. They accept. Time passes quickly and they go through the major cities of the state. When they arrive in Pesqueira, the mayor bids them farewell and disembarks.

The remaining route (fifteen miles) between Mimoso and the headquarters is made smoothly and safely. The major and the Colonel of Rio Branco remain silent most of the time. When the train arrives in Mimoso, the major bids farewell and disembarks. Upon leaving, it shows on his face how happy he is as he has returned successful.

Arranged Marriage

After greeting the station officials, the major heads for his house. He sees some people along the way but doesn't pay much attention because he's thinking on how best to break the news to his women. What would Christine's reaction be? What would his beloved wife say? The first had betrayed his confidence by dating a simple tax collector. The second still wished her daughter was a nun. Well, he didn't care. He was the man of the house and the two would have to abide by his decisions. What he decided was best for the whole family. With that thought, the major hurries and before long arrives home. He opens the front door and heads to the living room but there's no one there. He calls his daughter and wife and they respond from the kitchen. Quickly, he heads there.

— I've returned from Recife. Won't you hug me?

Christine and Helena warmly respond to the major's request. They exchange caresses a while.

— I bring good news for you. Look, what an honor, I had the privilege of speaking with the governor in person.

— I always knew you were a great man. Since I met you I knew you were the man of my life. A man of vision and success. You bought the rank of major, we moved to Recife and you had the bright idea to get hold of much of the land located west of Pesqueira. Ever since then, we've had many accomplishments. I'm proud of you, my love. (Helena)

The major and his wife hug and kiss and Christine is thrilled with the scene. She also wanted to be as happy as her parents were.

— What news do you have, father? I'm dying to know.

The major asks them to sit with a serious and mysterious look on his face.

— Well, there are two big announcements. The first is that the governor will give his full support to my candidacy for mayor of the city of Pesqueira. The second, and no less important, is that I have planned a nice marriage for you, Christine. Your husband will be the son of the important Colonel of Rio Branco. His name is Bernardo and he is the same age as you. The wedding will be in a month.

A cold chill runs down Christine's spine and she gets a little dizzy. Had she heard correctly? This reality was worse than any nightmare.

— What? You've arranged a marriage for me? I wasn't expecting that. Father, I'm not ready for it. I don't even know this guy much less love him. Please forgive me, but I'm not going to marry him.

— I am also opposed to it. I always dreamed that she become a nun. I still have hope that she will go back to the convent. Marriage will not bring happiness to my daughter.

— It is decided. You thought I was going accept you flirting around with Claudio? Not even in his wildest dreams could he ever be my son-in-law. I didn't raise my daughter to give herself to just anyone. As for love, don't worry, you'll acquire it over time.

Christine starts crying about the whole situation. Did that mean he already knew about her and Claudio? He hadn't said anything.

—Father, I love Claudio with all my might. Even if I can't be with him, I wouldn't forget him. This marriage that you arranged for me will only bring unhappiness. I feel that this will not end well.

— Nonsense. Everything is going to be all right. As for Claudio, he will no longer do you any more harm. I've taken him out of...circulation.

— What did you do with him?

— I told Deputy Pompeu to arrest him. There, he will regret the day he touched you.

— You're a heartless monster. I hate you!

Christine leaves the kitchen and goes and locks herself in her room. She would cry the rest of the day for her impossible love.

Visit

The arrival of a new day didn't seem to be animating Christine. She had just woke up but remained motionless on the bed. The previous day had been devastating in her life. With the news of the arranged marriage, her heart was destroyed and her hopes of being happy too. She could only think of Claudio and his suffering. She tries to get up but her weakened body resists the attempt. She tries once, twice, three times until she can get up. She looks in the mirror and sees a felled and defeated Christine. What would become of her? Could she hide the disgust she felt for this stranger who was going to marry her? After all he was destroying a beautiful love story. She reflects better and changes her opinion. The two weren't to blame. The archaic system that says that parents should arrange marriages for their children was to blame. Where was the idolized freedom conceived in the French Revolution? It simply did not exist in Brazil. Equality and fraternity were also distant goals to be achieved. In a world where the colonels and authoritarians ruled there was no place for human rights.

Christine walks away from the mirror and decides to take a bath. Maybe a bit of cold water would sooth her nerves and her mood? It is with that hope that she goes into the bathroom. About twenty minutes later she comes out looking to be a little better. Water really has the ability to restore forces. She dries herself off and puts on a nice outfit. Soon after, she goes to have breakfast in the kitchen. She finds her mother being served by Gerusa.

— Where is father?

— He left early. He went to buy cattle on the farm nearby. Later, he has a business meeting in at the Residents' Association. (Helena)

— Is he still fixed on the idea of wanting to have me married?

— He was very clear yesterday. Your wedding is scheduled for next month. If I were you I would learn to accept it because he won't change his mind.

— You, my mother, could not appeal for me? This marriage won't bring anything good for our family.

— I don't want to fight with your father. Our marriage has lasted so long because I knew how to be cautious and submissive. If you had listened to me and stayed in the convent, you would not be facing this situation. You would be right in this very moment, in full communion with our Lord Jesus Christ.

— I wasn't going to live your dream, mother. I have my own life. There are many other ways to serve our Lord Jesus Christ.

— Then don't ask anything of me.

Christine was quiet and finished having breakfast. She gets up and invites Gerusa to accompany her on a walk, and she readily agrees. The two leave in order not to arouse the suspicions of Helena. When they are outside of the house, Christine passes on instructions to the maid. She accepts and the two continue to walk. They were heading to the police station where Christine intended to see, if only briefly, her great love, Claudio. She was devastated thinking about the atrocities to which they were submitting him. She hastens her steps, looking forward to seeing him. She had not forgotten the moments on the mountain or Sucavão where she surrendered herself totally. Her father could marry her to another man but it wouldn't kill the feeling she carried in her heart. Not even if he wanted to, he couldn't do that.

Sometime later they finally get to the police station. Christine orders Gerusa to wait outside and she heads to the office of the delegate.

— What a very good morning, Miss Christine, what do you want?

— I want to speak with the inmate, Claudio.

— I'm sorry but I have strict orders that he is not to receive visits from anyone. By the way, his parents were here and I sent them off. He is held with no visitors.

— You know very well that his arrest is illegal. If the authorities of the municipality find out, you are in big trouble.

— Really, the only authority I know is your father, the major. That man is terrible, if you forgive me for saying so.

— You don't understand me. I want to see him now or are you going to refuse to answer a request from the daughter of the major?

Delegate Pompeu thought about it for a while and decided not to risk it. He called one of his subordinates and ordered them to leave Claudio alone with Christine, in a reserved room. The two embraced and they kissed at length.

— How are you? Are they hurting you?

— I'm beat up. Being away from you is the greatest of all torment. The treatment and food are not good but I am alive. You were right Christine; your parents are very biased.

Christine passes her hand on Claudio's back and realizes there are marks of his suffering visible. A shiver runs through her body and she starts to cry.

— Why did all this have to happen? Why can't two humans have the right to love freely? And the request we made to mountain? Will it come true some day?

— Have faith in love and in the mountain, Christine. As long as we're alive, there is hope, however small. We went into the cave of despair, even if it was in our imaginations, and we beat the obstacles and traps. The cave is able to make the deepest desires come true.

— Yes, it's true. Often, in my imagination, I have gone into parallel planes where only the two of us reside. I see myself married with seven of your beautiful children.

— That's the way. However, you shouldn't have risked so much by coming here. This place stains your beauty. I'm going to be all right, don't worry. If you see either of my parents, please tell them that I miss them.

— I took a chance because I love you. Never forget it. I will be praying to Saint Sebastian, the brave soldier, asking for your freedom.

— Thank You. I love you, too.

The two hug, kiss and finally say goodbye. Time was up. Upon leaving the room, Christine thanks the delegate and goes away. Gerusa is outside, waiting. Christine gives her a few more instructions and the two go back home.

The Beating

Major Quintino is in a business meeting in the building of the Residents' Association. He gestures, proposing agreements and listens to complaints from the members of the association. His rank of major gave him the right to have the last word. In the middle of the meeting, Delegate Pompeu shows up asking for five minutes of his attention. He excuses himself and goes to talk to him outside of the association.

— What is so important that you had to interrupt the meeting? Couldn't you wait to talk to me later? (Major)

— I came to inform you that your daughter showed up at the police station demanding to speak with the inmate Claudio.

— What? You didn't allow it, did you?

— She insisted so much, I gave in. After all, she's your daughter.

— You really are incompetent. Had I not given the order not to let anyone visit? The only reason you are not immediately removed from your post is because you've already serviced the community relevantly. As of today, do not allow him to receive any more visitors, not even if it's the Pope himself. My daughter let me down once more. I think I have to take serious action.

— I will comply, sir. Thank you for not firing me.

— You're dismissed. I have heard enough.

The major bids farewell to the delegate and returns to the association building to let them know he was leaving. Some people complain but he doesn't care. Stunned, he heads to his home where Christine awaits, innocently. Flurries of thoughts fill the confused mind of the major. He recalls the betrayal by Christine and his blood boils even more. Who did she think she was dealing with? With a comprehensive and loving father? She didn't even wait for the major's reaction. He remembers Christine's reaction upon learning of the arranged marriage and how she misunderstood. The zeal for his family and the future of his daughter took first place for him. He would climb over any obstacles to achieve his goals. Even if that meant he lost the love and affection of his only daughter. She would thank him, later, in the future. Sometime after the major arrives home, opens the front door and enters. The first person he sees is his wife, Helena.

— Where is Christine?

— She's in her room, resting.

— Call her immediately. I want to speak with her.

Helena knocks on the door of her room and calls her. Moments later she appears and faces the major.

— It's you whom I want to speak to. What's this I hear about you talking with Claudio? Do you not understand that you two have no future?

— My heart told me to meet with him and see how he was. You can force me to marry another man but not erase what I feel for him. Our love is eternal.

— You will pay dearly for having gone up against me. I'm the major, the highest decision-making authority of this region, and not even you, my daughter, can go against my will. Listen carefully: As of today, I forbid you to leave without my permission and I will do something I should have done a long time ago.

The major unravels the leather belt that is on his pants and with a fast move grabs Christine with one of his strong, masculine arms. Christine tries to escape but can't. Mercilessly, he begins to deal serious blows to her with the belt. Christine screams in pain and her mother, Helena tries to save her. The major threatens her and she moves away. He keeps beating Christine for a while and when he realizes that it's enough, he stops. Christine falls exhausted and wounded on the ground. Helena comes to her aid and the major retires. Christine cries, not from pain, but from finding out that her father is a heartless scoundrel. She doesn't regret anything that she did nor the love she felt for Claudio. She was willing to suffer for something she considered to be sacred. The major's beatings and threats didn't prevent her from dreaming about her true love. After all, what meaning would life have if she lost hope of being happy? For love, she'd risk losing her life if necessary.

Helena helps Christine take a shower and then to collect herself in her room. She was in no condition to receive anyone or partake in any activity.

Gerusa's Cousin

Mimoso had received a new inhabitant who was just arriving at the train station. It was Clemilda, Gerusa's cousin. Originally from Bahia, her birth had been surrounded by mysteries. She had been born at the exact moment when her mother was participating in an occult ritual tribute. Ever since she was born, the girl showed a certain natural ability in dealing with these forces. Fearing her gifts, her mother abandoned her shortly after at the door of a charitable institution. She was rescued by employees and raised as their daughter. Since her adoption, mysterious occurrences began to happen at that same institution. Glass and mirrors broke frequently, fires occurred without apparent reason and the sound of claws could be heard on the roof and on the windows. In one of those fires, she was the only child to escape. The institution was closed and she had become an orphan again. She was then snatched up by a homeless man and began practicing petty crime to survive. Her gifts were discovered and her benefactor began using it to his benefit to amass wealth. She grew up cheating, stealing and tampering with lottery results. Shortly after her benefactor died and she was free of his influence. She was alone in Salvador. She then decided to write a letter to her cousin Gerusa (who visited her regularly and was the only family that she had ever met) telling her the situation. She invited her to come live in Mimoso, where she worked as a maid in a wealthy home. Clemilda readily accepted.

She now was there, at the station, fully convinced and reassured of her decision. She would put her plan into action soon as she had total control over the occult forces. Mimoso would be the ideal place for her kingdom of injustice. After conquering Mimoso, she intended to take over the world. However, for this to happen, she would have to unbalance the "opposing forces" and use them to her advantage.

The steps to accomplish this were to deploy a curse, distort a true love and cause a tragedy. With everything complete, she could stifle the true religion and take control of everything.

She checks the address contained in her letter and asks a person nearby how to get there. She is directed by the person and starts walking. Her thoughts are full of negative energy and she only thinks about destroying, humiliating and perverting. In her suitcase, she carries an oracle which serves as an intermediary between her and the God of Darkness. She remembers her first contact with the underworld and how she felt happy and powerful for achieving such a feat. After that, she had numerous contact. The last message she received had clarified certain facts unknown to her. Now she was ready to take action and start her kingdom of injustice.

She continues walking and soon sees the beautiful bungalow. She feels a mixture of anguish and suffering inside the house. She laughs as she takes pleasure in these situations. She walks a little faster and soon comes to the house. She claps and yells to be attended to. A few moments pass and Gerusa comes to answer the door.

— My cousin, Clemilda. How good it is to see you here.

— I arrived a little while ago. You've got a place for me?

— Not yet. The major's home and you can talk to him personally. Please, come in.

Clemilda accepted the invitation immediately. She enters the house (accompanied by Gerusa) and goes to talk to the major. She finds him in the living room.

— Mr. Major, this is my cousin, Clemilda, who comes from Bahia. She came to speak with your grace.

— Nice to meet you. My name is Quintino and as you probably already know, I am the greatest political authority in this region. What do you want?

— My cousin Gerusa invited me to come and live here in Mimoso because I was alone in Salvador. I was wondering if you, sir, could get me a good job and also a place to live.

— Well, one of my houses is unoccupied and seeing as how you are Gerusa's cousin, and she's been with us so many years, I can give it to you. About the job, nothing comes to mind right now but when I see a good opportunity I'll let you know. Was that all? Gerusa will give you the keys to the house. In fact, it is a gigantic castle. I think you might like it.

— That's all. Thank you.

Glad to have gotten accommodations, the witch left for her new home. The next day would be the beginning of her cruel plan.

The "Blessing"

One day after Clemilda's arrival, the residents of the beautiful bungalow are having breakfast. Christine avoids talking to her father as she is still resentful of the beating she took. Helena and the major talk freely.

— You mean that the boy doesn't want to come meet our daughter? I find this absurd. (Helena)

— His father prefers it that way. It is to maintain a certain air of mystery. It is a pity that our daughter is not enjoying the idea of getting married. I would give anything to convince her that it is the best. (Major)

— Forget it. Don't ask for the impossible.

Gerusa overhears and decides to intervene.

— I know someone who can help. My cousin Clemilda is experienced in relationships.

— I think it's a good idea. Gerusa, accompany my daughter to the home of Ms. Clemilda. If you succeed, I will reward you. (Major)

— I'm not going. (Christine)

— You don't have to want to. Do not make me whip you again. (Major)

A shudder runs through Christine's body remembering the punishment. She was not willing to experience that feeling again. She agrees despite it not being her own will. She gets up from the table and accompanies Gerusa. The two leave the house and can already see Clemilda's residence, which sits just across the street. A chill is felt by Christine as a warning that she shouldn't go. However, the fear of her father was greater and she decided to keep quiet. The few feet leading to the residence were covered. Gerusa knocks on the door to be met. In a few moments Clemilda appears.

— I was waiting for you. Come in. You are Christine, are you not?

— How do you know me, ma'am?

— Everyone comments about you. They talk about your beauty and your good ways. I just assumed when you arrived. Well, come in.

Gerusa and Christine enter and the environment was full of negative vibes. The objects that had previously made up the horror scene had already been removed by Clemilda.

— I brought Christine here for you to advise her to accept the marriage that the major has arranged. She is resistant to this idea.

— Well, I think I can talk to her. Gerusa, can you leave us alone a moment? By the way, there is a stack of things to be washed in the kitchen.

— You never change. Always trying to exploit me.

Gerusa obeys and goes to the kitchen. Clemilda approaches Christine and starts to circle around her.

— I see a man in your path. His name is Claudio, isn't it? He is a young man, muscular and beautiful. You met at work and the seed of love was deposited in your heart. However, think with me, why wouldn't he be interested in you? You are young, beautiful, intelligent and above all, the daughter of a powerful major. Could it be that the love that you feel is not reciprocated? I guarantee you that he would have his reasons: pride, ambition and power. That's what people look for. The love you have drawn in your heart is just an illusion.

— You're not going to convince me that easily. I know Claudio and what we feel is real. I don't need to read his mind to be sure of his feelings. Illusion is this marriage that they got me into.

— Have you considered that it can merely be a plan of his? Don't you think it's strange the sudden friendship you've started? People are really predictable. What they want is to end up on top, regardless of the feelings of others.

— Your poisonous mouth won't confuse me. I shouldn't have come here as I don't feel well.

— Hold on, dear. Let me bless you so that you will be happy in your marriage.

Before Christine could respond, Clemilda put her hand on her head. She spoke unintelligible words and Christine started getting dizzy. A whirlwind of energy jumped out of her hands and into Christine's head. The operation lasted little more than thirty seconds. Later, Christine took her hand off and called for Gerusa. She answered; the two left the residence and returned home. The blessing had turned Christine into a mutant.

Phenomena

After the intriguing meeting with Clemilda the sorceress, Christine began to feel totally different than before. The usual activities she performed and which gave her pleasure such as knitting, reading and going to work had become tedious. What remained intact and was the only thing to do so, was the feeling she had for Claudio. In addition, strange phenomena began to happen around her. The knitting she learned as a child suddenly would not form anything. The lines no longer seemed to make any sense. While reading a book, the page she was reading was struck by a ray of fire and burned. She felt her eyes burning in that moment. Passing by metal objects, she would attract them. Every discovery, she became anxious and wondered what it all meant. Was it a curse? What she had become? No one could know or otherwise she would run the risk of being hospitalized and doctors from all over the world were going to experiment with her.

In order to avoid them finding out, she stopped going out with her friends and only participated in social activities strictly necessary such as work, for example. At all times, she sought to control herself because the phenomena only occurred when she was emotionally unstable. In order to get rid of the curse, she resorted to various methods but none of them proved effective. Bitter and angry, Christine increasingly isolated herself in her own world.

A New Friend

The routine of work, every fifteen days, was practically the only social activity that Christine took part in. Through it she met numerous people and made friends. Among them was a young girl, more or less the same age as Christine, named Rosa. The congeniality was mutual and every time they saw each other they spent a good time talking. On one such occasion, Christine asked her to come to her house and she readily accepted. On the day and at the time they had decided on, Rosa arrived, coming into the garden of the house, clapping to announce herself. Gerusa, the maid of the house, answered the door.

— How can I help you?

— I came to talk to Christine.

— Just a moment I'll go call her.

Sometime after, Christine shows up and invites her to go out with her on the porch of the house because it was the most ventilated and relaxing place to be.

— Well, Christine, I want to get to know you better. You told me earlier that you were going to be a nun. How was life in the convent?

— I spent three precious years of my life there. Well, the nuns were nice to me even though they were quite strict. The time dedicated to prayer was quite extensive and that bored me sometimes. I was of the opinion that if a human being wants to enter in contact with God it was not necessary to be so selfless and devoted because God is omniscient and understands everything we wish. Over time, they realized that I had no vocation and they kicked me out.

— So you left the cloister and returned to the world. You don't regret this decision?

— It all depends on how you look at it. Immediately, no. However, now that my father is forcing me to get married I think it would be better if I were there. Although that would just be me hiding away from an unfair world we live in where parents decide the futures of their children.

— Have you ever had a crush or fallen in love?

— When I was in the convent, I met a son of the gardener who captivated me. I thought it was love at that moment but soon after his abandonment I realized that it was just passion. True love I finally found with Claudio, my coworker. However, my parents' opposition made our relationship impossible. My only hope is the request I made on the mountain that everyone claims is sacred. Tell me a little about yourself. Have you ever loved someone?

— As I have said, I have a boyfriend named Felipe, the son of the owner of the warehouse. We both love each other and maybe one day we can get married. Our parents have totally supported us.

— I envy you. You don't know how much my parents' misunderstanding hurts me. I wish I was just a regular girl and not the daughter of the almighty major.

Tears pour down Christine's face and her friend tries to console her. The burden she carried on her back was too heavy for their immaturity. She wanted to be happy and saw the opportunity to be so slipping through her fingers. A mere two days remained for her to give herself over to a wedding without a future and to a stranger that she only knew by name. Seeing that her friend had no more desire to talk, Rosa said goodbye and promised to return another time. Their friendship was important for Christine as she didn't feel so isolated and completely abandoned.

The Day Before the Wedding

The proximity of the marriage caused Christine to become increasingly agitated. She had been talking with the priest, talking to a friend and had made one last attempt to convince her parents to give up the idea of marrying her off. So far, she hadn't gotten any results. The priest suggested that she resign and accept her situation. How could she do that? It was her life and happiness that were at stake. She learned, in the convent, that all human beings were free to make their own decisions and lead their own destinies. Her rights were being suppressed by a society in which children are married off by their parents. With her friend, she deliberated on her and Claudio's future. Neither had found a real and palpable alternative that could lead the two to be together other than the hope of the holy mountain and the request that Christine made to it. It was the only thing left for her to do; wait for a miracle or the unlikely to occur.

Christine goes towards the terrace and begins watching the sky. She remembers the moments spent on the mountain and the stars that she and Claudio observed together. They were witnesses to the feeling that united the two and even if the major and his social conventions would never allow it, the two would continue to love each other. Looking at the sky, she hopes the next world will be a fairer and better place and that those who really know true love can achieve happiness. She remembers God and how she learned how wonderful he is. She asks God to grant the wishes of the simplest dreamers without having to enter a cave or something else similar. She also asks for strength to endure her martyrdom to the end. She felt like a mutant and was disappointed in love. She cries the last tears she had left to cry and goes home.

Tragedy

It was finally daylight and this meant that the terrible day had arrived. Christine wakes up but tries to pretend to be asleep in order not to face reality. Who knew, they might forget her and maybe everything that she had suffered in the last few days had only been a simple nightmare? She wanted to open her eyes and find Claudio, her true love. She wanted to marry him, not a stranger, this son of the Colonel of Rio Branco. For a moment, she feels as if she's in Sucavão and recalls every detail of what happened there. She seems to be there feeling the force of the water, the manly embrace of Claudio and smelling his scent. She delves deep into this thought until a voice disturbs her and brings her back to reality. It was her mother.

— Christine, my daughter, wake up, the wedding guests are already arriving. Have you forgotten that it will be held at 8:00 AM?

— Oh, Mother, have patience. I barely slept the whole night thinking about this marriage.

Christine rises quite moody and goes to the bathroom to take a bath. Her mother is waiting in her room. About twenty minutes later she comes back and finds her beautiful dress spread out on the bed. She observes it and thinks it's pretty, although melancholy. Her mother helps her get dressed and put on makeup. With everything ready, she approaches the mirror to see how she looks. She sees a heartbroken version of herself, even though she is made up beautifully. She thinks about the idea of what was going to happen and about her future at the side of an unknown man. Suddenly, the mirror cracks and breaks, with a great snap. Christine screams and her mother rushes to the rescue. Fortunately, she didn't get hurt. She feels a pain in her chest and wonders what's going to happen. She remembers her reoccurring dreams. Her mother calms her and says it's nothing. The two go into the living room to meet the family of the groom and receive some guests. The major takes Christine's hand and begins to introduce her.

— Mr. Henrique, this is my daughter Christine. Isn't she beautiful?

— Yes, she's very beautiful. My son is a lucky man. Today will complete the union of our families and this makes me very happy.

Christine forces a laugh in order not to be unpleasant. The mother of the groom also tries to be nice.

— After you are married if you need any help, don't hesitate to ask me. The women of our family are very close.

Karina, the sister of the groom, steps forward also and praises Christine's hair. The Major and Helena welcome their guests that are still arriving. When the clock strikes exactly 8:00 AM everyone goes out to the terrace where the marriage will take place. Christine is walked, by the major, to the makeshift altar. On her way to the altar, she has the opportunity to see, at a glance, faces with anxious expressions. She sees the Mother Superior and the nuns who had lived with her in the convent. She also sees her first professors and her cousins who came from Recife. All in all, she can sense the anticipation and excitement of the moment. Moving forward a little more, she can already see the groom and Father Chiavaretto. Suddenly, a rage inside her takes over her and makes her hate both of them. Why had that man named Bernardo agreed to marry her? After all, he was a man and had more freedom of action. She would surrender herself to a marriage with no future and would be unhappy for the rest of her life. What about the Father? How did he get locked into participating in that farce? The church should have stood by her and been her accomplice rather than accept the situation.

She gets closer to the groom and her anger does not diminish. Upon seeing him, a ray of lightning comes straight from her eyes and hits him right in the chest. He falls over, dead. The commotion in the audience stirs and Christine falls at his feet.

— She's a monster! (Some scream)

The major acts fast and sends his henchmen to help Christine rise up and protect her from the angry crowd. Meanwhile, the nuns cross themselves, not believing what they had just seen. The groom's family tries to pressure the delegate to take action but the major rejects his actions. In the end, Christine is saved and the major sends the guests away. The party and all festivities are canceled. The arranged marriage had resulted in a tragedy.

The Black Cloud

With the tragedy completed, Clemilda began to cast a spell that would reach the entire region of Mimoso. She had the authority to do this because she had fulfilled the three steps: She had set a curse, had distorted true love and caused a tragedy. Now, the ministry of the unholy was ready for action, suffocating Christianity. She gets close to the cauldron and puts the last ingredients in it for her spell. Pronouncing unintelligible words, she dances around it. Suddenly, she stops and says with a deep, strong voice: -Dark cloud, appear!

Immediately, a large, black, thick cloud covers the sky of Mimoso. The sun is also covered and with that the natural light of the sky decreases significantly. The curse was programmed to take effect every day after 12:00 PM. With this, the witch would have her power doubled and could act more freely.

The Martyrs

Shortly after the deployment of the black cloud, the witch begins to act. She hired two pagans, Totonho and Cleide to assist her in her occult works. In addition, she instructed the two to get rid of the representatives of Christianity in the place. The first victims were Father Chiavaretto and the Friar Nunes, who was visiting Mimoso. In addition, some believers were decapitated and others put on stakes to burn in a bonfire. After the murders, they began destroying the small chapel which had been erected in honor of St. Sebastian. There was virtually nothing left but the cross that stood intact despite the attempts to destroy it. It was the symbol that Christianity was still alive and could react.

With the domination complete, the circle of "opposing forces" disbanded and it spawned an imbalance. If the situation remained like this for a long time, Mimoso would risk disappearing. That is because the forces of good would not remain captive before this sacrilege. In the end, this would result in an unpredictable war that could destroy both worlds.

End of the Vision

The sequence of images from the vision that filled my mind suddenly stopped. Consciousness gradually returns and I find myself holding a page of newspaper with the headline: Christine, the Young Monster. I observe it and think the headline woefully inadequate as the tragedy that happened was not in any way her fault. She was but another victim of the cruel and powerful sorceress Clemilda. Suddenly, I'm beginning to understand why my time travel and my victory over the cave came to be. I was part of a plot by destiny to try to retrieve the blessed Mimoso from the arms of tragedy. My mission was to reunite the "opposing forces" and help the owner of the scream heard in the cave. I was absolutely sure that the owner of that voice was the beautiful Miss Christine. A mutated, totally bitter Christine awaited me. I'd have to convince her to react and to make her my ally in the fight against the forces of evil. In the end, I'd have to remember the teachings of the guardian and the dreaded cave of despair, the cave that had realized my dreams and made me the Seer. I now had a new challenge and was willing to meet it.

With the newspaper in hand, I read the whole story about Christine. They claimed that she was a monster since childhood and that only then had it been discovered. A mixture of indignation and anger fill my whole being. How did those journalists have the courage to publish that? They had taken advantage of a tragedy in order to tell lies. Christine was never was, nor could be a monster either. She just had been cursed by an evil and perverse witch. It was up to good people to help her and heal her. I keep reading the paper and they claim that Christine was a young rebel who left the convent because of bad behavior. I'm revolted again. I feel like ripping up the whole newspaper. Damned journalists, they distort everything to make money. Christine was a young, submissive girl and had followed the advice of her mother to cloister herself in a convent. When the sisters realized that she had no vocation, they kicked her out. I quit reading the news because it was not true. The vision was enough for me to I know where I stood. I take the newspaper and return it to the cabinet drawer, next to the table, from where I had gotten it. I get up and start to draw up a plan of action in my mind. I would have to somehow reunite the "opposing forces" and help Christine find true happiness. I approach the door and I am just about to open it.

Testimony

When it opens, I'm surprised to see a gathering of people in the small foyer of the hotel. What was the meaning of all that? I get closer so that I can ask.

— What's going on here?

Pompeu, the delegate, speaks up.

— We're here because serious allegations were made against you. You need to come with us, boy.

The delegate signals to his underlings and they bring handcuffs. They put them on my wrists and I feel wronged, like a slave back in the olden times. Carmen tries to intervene but the delegate doesn't listen.

— Is that really necessary? I have a clear conscience.

— We'll see about that at the station, son. (Major)

Obeying his orders, I begin to walk and the train leaves also. Upon leaving the hotel, I realize that there were a lot more people present, interested in what was going on. What did they want with me? Had I committed a crime? Ever since I arrived in Mimoso, I had tried very hard not to call attention to myself. However, now I was being handcuffed and taken to the police station. I'm starting to worry about what exactly to tell them. I could not tell the entire truth and jeopardize the mission. I would have to defend myself from the accusations with good common sense and intelligence. I begin to think of Claudio and the way he was thrown in jail. I would think of a way to avoid the same happening to me.

Some ten minutes after leaving the hotel, we finally arrive at the imposing police station. Major Quintino and Delegate Pompeu come in with me. The others are outside waiting for a decision. Upon entering the delegate's private office, they remove my handcuffs and with that I'm more relieved.

— Well, sit down, Mr. Seer. I am now the one who will ask the questions. First, what's your real name and where are you from? (Delegate)

— My name is Aldivan and I'm from Recife.

— What are you doing around here if you're from Recife? What's your profession?

— I'm a reporter for the Capital Newspaper and I came looking for a good story. I assure you, my intentions are the best possible. I'm not a criminal and I don't want to hurt anybody.

— What do you have to say about the relentless interrogations which you've been submitting the people of this place to? What exactly do you mean by doing this?

— It is part of my job, a strategy in which to collect information. However, if this has become awkward for anyone, I'll stop.

— As you may know, Queen Clemilda has made a decree against your person. What do you say to that? By chance, are you her enemy?

— I think I better not answer that question.

— Well, I have no further questions. Major, do you have any more questions you want to ask this guy?

— Yes. I want to know if he works for the opponents of the government.

— No, not at all. I'm not looking to get myself involved in political issues although I think the current system is quite unfair.

— Well, Mr. Aldivan, I think I'll let you stay in prison for a few days to check if everything that has been said here is true.

— I will not stay here. This is unfair. If you make this whimsical decision, I will denounce you to the governor who is a close friend of mine.

The major and the delegate are amazed by my reaction and by the news that I had just given. They gather to commune in silence and resolve not to risk it. In the end, I'm released despite the protests of some people outside the police station. My plan had worked.

Back to the Hotel

When I leave the station, I begin to wonder why the people of Mimoso have reacted so passively. They lived under the tyranny of a cruel witch and major. I think maybe it's fear that stops any retaliation from them. Suddenly, I begin to remember the three doors that I had to choose from in order to advance in the cave. They represented fear, failure and happiness. There, I learned to control my fears and confront them in spite of all the factors in the cave that likened to trip me up such as the dark, the unexpected and all of the pitfalls. I learned also to face failure not as the end but as the resumption of a new plan. I ended up choosing the door of happiness and it's what people don't often choose. Many are slaves to their daily lives, to egoism, to morality, shame and their own abilities to dream. Those are the ones who fail and are afraid. They don't even risk entering the cave to accomplish their desires. They become unhappy people with no self-love.

I look to my side. I see people who don't even know me yet who are very angry with my release from the police station. At the bottom of their hearts they have already judged and sentenced me. How often do we do that? How often do we think we own the truth and that we have the power to condemn? Remember what Jesus said: Remove first the beam out of thy own eye before pointing it at thy brother. He said that because we all have flaws and this makes our judgments partial and obscure. Only those who know the human heart and who are free from all sin have the ability to see everything clearly. I look for the last time at these people and I feel sorry for them because they prefer their greedy sense of justice rather than reflecting on their own lives. I leave them behind and continue on my way back to the hotel. I start to mentally organize every step that I would make in order to reunite the "opposing forces" and help Miss Christine. She had been the owner of that scream that I heard in the cave of despair and that led me to travel through time. This journey was part of a process of spiritual and human improvement for me and at the same time had the purpose of correcting injustices. I keep walking and after about five minutes I get to the hotel. Renato and Carmen are waiting at the gate. They are my companions in this fight. The next day would be the most appropriate time to start my plans.

The Idea

The first rays of sun caress my face and the force of natural light has just awakened me. I remain immobile for a while because I didn't have such a good night. I was still remembering the nightmare I had last night which made me wake up. In the dream, I was with some young people talking about my book. I spoke of my expectations and the hopes of getting a commercial publisher for it. Along comes a little devil bothering and scaring everyone. People fled and the demon, who did not show his face, exclaimed: -So you have it all figured out!

In that moment, the nightmare ends and I wake up in the middle of the night, sweating profusely. What did this mean? Did it have something to do with the history of Mimoso? I wasn't sure. What I did know is that I wanted to have a decent place in the universe and if my destiny and my vocation were in literature, I would follow it with great passion. After all, why had I entered the cave if I was not to become the Seer, someone able to transcend time, predict the future and understand the most confused and distressed hearts? With that thought, I turn in bed and stand up. I observe Renato who is still asleep and wonder why the guardian had insisted so much about me bringing him with me. Up until now he had barely contributed. What could a child do for me? Well, I didn't know. I divert my attention from him and I head to the bathroom to quickly bathe. The bath would leave me more accessible. I enter, turn on the water, and start to feel the benefits already. I think of my family and I am feeling homesick. I remember my mother and my sister and how they were so contrary to my dream. A feeling of forgiveness invades my being and I end up forgetting this fact. After all, it was I who had to believe in my own talent and calling. In addition to washing my body, I try to clear my mind of any impurities because I had to be prepared to overcome the obstacles and challenges that may appear. I turn off the water and soap up.

At that moment a small drop, by itself, touches my head and I travel instantly through distant dimensions. I see myself in heaven, talking with angels and asking them what the meaning of life is. In response, I hear ringing and this leaves me more confused. After the angels, I talk with the Apostles and one of them tells me I'm very special to God. He considers me his son. I see, from a distance, the Virgin and she looks the same to me as the other times I've seen her: pure and wise. After, I see Jesus Christ on his throne, with all his glory, and he tells me to be good and to trust my talent. All this had happened in less than one second, the time that it took the drop of water to touch my head. Then I see the faucet, the water running down my body, and I come back to reality. I decide to turn it off because I'm clean enough. Coming out of the bathroom, I find Renato still asleep and I am upset. I shake his body vigorously in order to wake him up. He gets up grumbling and goes to take a bath. I take this opportunity to go to the kitchen of the hotel and have breakfast. When I arrive, I'm well received by all and Carmen serves me some snacks.

— You mean that yesterday the delegate released you just like that? (Rivanio)

— I was able to convince him. He had no reason to keep me imprisoned there.

— You got lucky, boy. It is common in this village for many injustices to occur. An example is Claudio. He's arrested because he became involved with the major's daughter. (Gomes)

— It's really a shame. If I could do something for him...

— You better not dare. The major would consider you his enemy and that would be a nightmare. The methods that the major uses to deal with his enemies are not pleasant. (Carmen)

The warning from Carmen left me quite reflective. I had to really be careful because the major and the witch weren't to be kidded with. I was treading in enemy territory and would have to play the right moves in order to come out a winner. The conversation continues on to other subjects and I finish my breakfast. As soon as I finish, Carmen calls me for a private conversation.

— Well, it's time to discuss payment as I had stated earlier. Do you have money?

The question caught me a little by surprise but I remembered that I had brought some with me on the trip. I excused myself, looked in my bag and came back with some change. Carmen took the money and asked;

— Which country is this money from? I have never heard of "Reais." Unfortunately, I cannot accept it. I want national currency.

The response of Carmen was like a slap in the face and then I realized that in 1910 my money had no value. I had no response.

— Well, I see you don't have any money. Then you will have to get a job to pay me. How about if you work for the major as a journalist?

— I don't think that's a good idea. However, it's the only option I have. I'm going to talk to the major and ask for a job.

— That's the way. I wish you good luck.

Carmen gives me a hug and retires. Her idea was not so bad. I would have the opportunity to meet Christine and who knows, maybe even have some kind of contact with her.

The Figure of the Major

Shortly after having spoken with Carmen and her having given me the idea, I decided to set it all up. After all, the clock was ticking and I had now just over two weeks to gather the "opposing forces" and help Christine find her destiny. With that in mind, I went to my room, put good clothes on and left. Upon leaving the hotel, I begin to concentrate and think about the best way to treat the major because he was a difficult man, very prejudiced, proud and overbearing. Christine and Claudio were some of the victims of his way of thinking and acting. I didn't want to become one more and would need to choose the right words. I continue to reflect on the major and think of the numerous difficulties he went through when he was just a child. However, he did not seem to have learned anything since he couldn't miss an opportunity to humiliate and harm people. Life had hardened his heart and his soul. He wasn't anyone's idea of a perfect boss but I needed the job to carry out my plans.

For a moment, I stop thinking about it and speed up a little because I'm near the bungalow. I look around me and the people that I see are sad and conformed. I think the people of Mimoso are partly responsible for the current situation of tyranny and injustice that occurs in this place. They were dominated by a wicked witch and by the major representative of the Colonel System. One threatened the people with black magic and the other used force to intimidate and bully. Both could be overturned if all united in rebellion against them. A lack of initiative and conformism kept them in the same situation, dominated. So the forces of good took action and made me travel to a mountain that everybody said was sacred. There, I met the guardian, the young girl, the ghost, the boy, performed three challenges and entered a cave capable of making the deepest of dreams come true. In the cave, I escaped traps and I advanced scenarios until I reached the end. I was transformed into the Seer and I traveled in time chasing a voice I didn't know. It was the voice of Miss Christine, the recently changed daughter of the major. A major who I would now face in order to get a job and pay what I owed Carmen. Finally, I come to the bungalow and the maid of the house comes to greet me in the garden.

— How may I help you, sir?

— My name is Aldivan and I'm a journalist. I want to talk to the major. Is he home?

— Yes. Come in, he's in the living room.

With my heart racing, I enter the beautiful bungalow. My anxiety and nervousness were killing me. I go into the room and greet the major.

— What brings you here, Mr. Seer?

— Well, as your Excellency knows, I'm a journalist. So I thought that your Excellency might need my services and I decided to come here to review my contract.

— Look, I don't know you well and I'm still not sure if you're a spy or if you belong to the opposition. I don't think I can help you.

— I guarantee I'm trustworthy and a major like you needs journalistic support to be approved by society. It is as the saying goes, the media is who creates a man.

— Looking at it that way, I think it might be a good idea. Let's do an experiment to see if it works. However, if you harm my image you will be treated as an enemy and you may have heard that this is not by any means a comfortable thing to have happen. As for salary, it will be good money. You need not worry.

— Thank You. I promise not to disappoint you. When do I begin?

— Get to work as soon as possible. I want to see my name circulated throughout Pernambuco. I want to be legendary and remembered by many generations.

— It will be so, Major. I promise you.

I bid farewell and leave. With the mission accomplished, I feel more relaxed and confident. Convincing the major had not been so difficult because he was thirsty for power and fame. I had played into his weakness and so I came out a winner.

The Job

The major gave me my first instructions and I started working to advance his name. Basically, my job was to strengthen him by disseminating his acts and favors to the local population and contribute to his campaign when he would run for mayor of the municipality. These assignments did not put me in a comfortable position because I was totally contrary to the ideals of the Colonel System and the attitude of the major. However, I knew this was the only chance to get close to Christine as she was completely reserved after the tragedy. My motto was: It is the end that justifies the means. One of the first articles of news that I had to disclose was as follows: the major helping needy families. I specified the date, spoke of the goodness of the major and his actions, and I mentioned the thanks of the people and the catastrophic situation that they were in. However, the most important thing was not disclosed. I didn't mention that the money used to buy the food baskets came from taxes and that in return the major required the families to vote for him for mayor. The act of "kindness" was nothing but a game of interest which was very popular during the rule of the Colonel System. I now became an accomplice of this system even against my own will. I try not thinking about it anymore and keep working. My strategy now was to find a way to communicate with Christine and let her find her own destiny.

The First Encounter with Christine

With a lot of material produced I approach the bungalow where the major lives. His approval was required for further publication of the work. Along the way, ideas come to me and I figure I would mention them to him. I think better of it and end up giving up the idea because the major was a hard man and generally did not accept suggestions. I walk a few more steps and finally I come to the residence. When I clap, a beautiful girl comes to greet me.

— What do you want, sir?

— I have come to speak with the major.

— He's not here. Can you come another time?

— No problem. May I speak with you? You are Miss Christine, aren't you?

— Yes. My name is Aldivan and I'm a reporter for the Capital Newspaper. I work for your father.

— Oh, my father has spoken about you. You're doing articles about him, aren't you?

— Yes. In addition, I am interested in your story. Could we talk for a minute?

— My story? I think that it doesn't concern you.

— I insist. I can help you find yourself. Give me the opportunity.

Suddenly, Christine's eyes fix on mine and our chains of thought unite. In a few moments, she has the opportunity to get to know me a little better. She thinks awhile and decides.

— All right, I'm going to get two chairs for us to sit down here on the porch.

She enters the house and comes back shortly after. She sits next to me and I can smell her delightfully natural scented perfume.

— Well, Christine, what caught my attention was the news I read in the paper in Recife recently. It spoke of a tragedy and about you as a person.

— What is written is true and was reported throughout Pernambuco. I'm a monster! I'm a monster! I ended that boy's life. He was a victim of that situation just like I was. Now, after the tragedy, I'm alone and everyone runs away from me. I don't have any more friends, not even God. I'm at rock bottom.

— Don't say that, Christine. If you feel guilty then stop because what happened was a sordid plot of the forces of evil represented by Clemilda. They took everything from you, even your God. If you react, there may be hope.

— How do you know all this? Who are you really?

— If I tried to explain it to you now, you wouldn't understand. I want you to know that, in me, you have a great friend, forever. You are no longer alone.

Tears pour down Christine's face with my sincerity. She hugs me and says she's been lacking in affection lately. I try to restart the conversation.

— Tell me, how was your experience at the convent. Did you find God there?

— Yes, I did. However, we can find God anywhere. He's in the water of the waterfall that descends, completely delivered to its destination, He's in the singing of the birds at daybreak, and He is in the gesture of the mother who protects her son. Anyway, he's inside of us and asks to be heard continuously. When I figured this out and learned to listen to him I understood that my vocation was not that of being a nun. I learned that I could serve Him in other ways.

— I admire you for this gesture and I agree with your definition. How many people deceive themselves their whole lives and give themselves up to paths in life that are not for them.

Sometimes, this happens under the influence of parents, society, or just not knowing how to listen to that inner voice that we all have and that you call God. Since you decided to leave the religious life, I assume you have found love.

— Yes, but I don't want to talk about it. It still hurts so much, the tragedy, and all the events preceding it.

I resolve to respect Christine's silence and dare not ask her anything more. I say farewell and ask if we could talk some other time. She says yes and that makes me happy. My first encounter with Christine had been a success.

Return to the Castle

After the first encounter with Christine, I decided to again face the powerful sorceress Clemilda. She had to know that the forces of good were at work and that the Ministry of Evil was coming to an end. With this in mind, I go again to the dreaded black castle. It has the same aspect as the time before and I start shivering, breathing irregularly and my heart was rather accelerated. What kind of mystique was this? The "opposing forces" were shouting within me. While getting closer, troubled and confused voices try to get me off of my path. I kneel on the floor and try to clear my mind to proceed. The voices are really strong. I begin to remember the teachings of the guardian, the challenges and the cave. I also remember my meditation and how it helped me. I apply what I learned and start to feel better and I can continue. I get up and walk the last steps, finally arriving. The access door instantly opens and without fear I go through it. The horror scene of the time before repeats itself but I don't pay any more attention to it. Firm and resolute, I go to the hallway where I am greeted by Totonho, one of Clemilda's cronies. He sends me to a room. Inside, in the center, is Clemilda wearing a hood.

— To what do I owe the honor of another visit from the Seer? Have you come to congratulate the work that I do in this rustic place?

— Don't start with me. You know, even more than I, that the imbalance in the "opposing forces" is threatening Mimoso and even the universe. I want you to leave here as soon as possible. The hurt you have caused people, particularly a young girl named Christine is too much. I'm glad that I became friends with her and I'm starting to make her see her own destiny.

— I doubt you'll be able to convince her to be a confident, totally guilt-free, young girl. The tragedy affected her senses and feelings. About the "opposing forces," you're right, but it won't be easy to get me out of here. I propose a deal. If you persuade Christine to really change her course and if you complete three challenges on three different days you'll be entitled to a final battle. The "opposing forces" will meet and face each other, and whoever wins will rule for eternity.

— A battle? Isn't it dangerous? The universe is in danger of disappearing if something goes wrong.

— You have no choice. It's take it or leave it. Do you really want to save Mimoso? Then face the force of "Darkness."

— Deal. I'll do it.

Having said that, I retired from the room and searched for the exit. A war was about to begin between the "opposing forces" and I was one of the main characters of this confrontation. I didn't know what was going to happen but I was willing to do anything to reverse the imbalance of "opposing forces" and help Christine.

The Message II

The meeting with Clemilda let me know that I had to act immediately and put my plan into action. The war between the "opposing forces" was declared and I had a major role in it. So I decided to write a note, addressed to Christine, inviting her for another meeting. After I wrote it I called Renato and asked him to deliver the note into her very hands. He took it and left without delay. About twenty minutes later he came back, bringing along with him the answer. I grab the paper carefully and open it slowly as if I am afraid of the answer. It contains the following message: Meet me at 7:00 AM at the road to Climério. I'm glad to hear that she accepted the invitation and my hopes of recuperating her increase. She was a key player in the fight against the force opposing us.

Trip to Climério

The day of the meeting was finally here. I get up and arrange the most appropriate strategy to be used at the meeting. I go to the bathroom and take a bath, brush my teeth and go to have breakfast. After completing all of these steps I'm ready to go out and find Christine. The meeting place I knew well. It was in Climério, located east of Mimoso. With the disposition that I had woken up with, I start walking towards the meeting place. It was past 7:00 AM and exactly at this time Christine should have already left her house. The memory of our first encounter comes to mind and I wonder if Christine trusts me already because she was plenty retracted during the first moments of the interview. Well, no wonder. I was a stranger, a stranger that turned out to be extremely knowledgeable of the details of her life. This generates an unprecedented impact. I'm glad that I had stated clearly that I wanted to be her friend and seeing how she felt extremely lonely lately, she accepted, at least temporarily, my counsel and my advice. Now I was ready for the second stage which was the most important.

I walk for some time in the same direction and further along I see the figure of Christine. Immediately, I start running to meet her.

— How are you, Christine? Did you have a good night?

— Since the tragedy happened, I haven't had any good nights. I always dream about my marriage and everything that happened there. I don't know how long I'm going to live like this.

— You need to let it go, Christine. Forget the guilt and remorse because they only harm you. I learned that in life we must live in the present moment and forget our hurtful past. The good times are the ones we should remember in order to strengthen ourselves and continue walking with our heads held high.

— Those are just words. The pain I feel inside is still too much.

— One day you will overcome it. I'm sure of it. Well, Christine, I have something serious to talk to you about. It is about this witch Clemilda that invoked the powers of darkness to take over the village of Mimoso. She was responsible for the tragedy and all the other bad events here since then. I confronted her and I am determined to end her reign. In response, she offered me a deal. Now, I need to gather the "forces of good" for a battle. What do you say? Are you ready to defend me in this fight?

— I don't know if I'm ready. Clemilda is Gerusa's cousin and Gerusa was practically a mother to me. I know she's bad and I'm totally against her actions. On the other hand, she's practically family. It's the "opposing forces" that confuse my heart and leave me in doubt.

— I understand. I must remind you that you have a key role in the war to come. Before you decide, think of the people, of Christianity and about yourself.

— I promise I will think about it. Want to tell me anything else?

I think a few moments before answering and I wonder if she's really ready. I decide to take the risk.

— Yes, the whole truth. Christine, for many years I was a young dreamer and full of hope. However, despite my best efforts I couldn't achieve my goals. I spent three years of my life completely deserted: I didn't have a job and I was not studying. Being at rock bottom led me to a crisis that almost drove me to madness. During this crisis, I tried to get closer to the Creator to obtain some peace and solace. However, the more I insisted, the less I received answers. So I tried to take refuge in the Devil looking for healing and answers. I went to a session and they promised me that I would be able to heal and be happy. In return, I would have to change religions and do exactly what they said. On the day and at the hour marked for my return back to this place I got the answer that God cared about me. He sent his Angel and warned me not to go back, that I would not find the much longed-for happiness and cure. So I heeded the warning and I dared not go back there. I saw a doctor and he said my case was not serious, that it was a simple nervous breakdown. So I took some medication and improved. God used that doctor to help me. How many times does he do so without us even realizing. During my crisis, I started to write to have a little fun, as therapy. Then I realized that I had a talent that I never noticed. After the crisis, I got a job and went back to school. At the same time, the desire to be a writer and to communicate with people was growing in me. That's when I heard about the Ororubá Mountain, the sacred mountain. It became sacred because of the death of a mysterious shaman, and it has a majestic cave at its top called the cave of despair. It is able to accomplish any dream, as long as it's pure and honest. So I decided to pack up and embark on a journey to the mountain. I said goodbye to my family but they didn't understand my dream. Nevertheless, I left. I had to believe in my own talent and potential. So I climbed the mountain and met the guardian, an ancient spirit. With her teachings, I was able to overcome the challenges that were my ticket into the cave. However, the story isn't finished. The cave of despair had never allowed anyone to carry out his or her dreams through it. All who have tried were summarily obliterated. However, I had a dream, and risking my life wouldn't be an obstacle for me. I decided to enter the cave. I started walking into it and soon, the first traps appeared. I managed to get rid of all of them and soon after, I came across three doors. They represented happiness, failure and fear. I picked the right door and I advanced in the cave. Then, I found a ninja and with his martial arts he tried to destroy me. The experience led me to victory and I felled the ninja. Then I advanced more in the cave and found a maze. I entered it and got lost. That's when I had an idea and I managed to find my way out. Then, I found a set of mirrors. This scenario made me reflect and helped me find myself. So I pushed a little farther into the cave. In short, I was able to advance all the scenarios of the cave and it saw itself obliged to grant my wish. I became the Seer and I traveled back in time, following a voice that I didn't know. This voice was yours, Christine, and I'm here to help you.

— That's a lot of information at once. I don't know if you're crazy or I'm losing my mind for hearing it. I already had heard of the cave and its wonderful powers but never imagined that someone had gone in and overcome its fire. I have to think a bit and reflect on all I heard.

— Think, Christine, but don't take too long. My time here is running out and I need to fulfill my mission.

— I promise to give you a response soon. Well, now I need to finish my walk and go back home.

I bid Christine farewell and I go back to the hotel. I had done my part, now all that was left was the answer. My hopes were in the hands of fate and I didn't know which way it pointed. The war between the "opposing forces" would occur soon and Christine's response would be the deciding factor.

Decision

The impending war between the "opposing forces" left me in no way assured. I had never participated in a contest of this type and it would be a unique experience. In order to relieve my heart and my mind, I leave the hotel and I direct myself to the ruins of the chapel of St. Sebastian, which is very close. Along the way, I wonder what challenges I'll face and if they'll be as difficult as the obstacles in the cave. Well, I would do everything in my power to win in the midst of any difficulties. My thoughts elevate and I think about my dream and every obstacle that it involves. I wonder if I'd get a commercial publisher for my book. Would the same invest enough for the book to achieve success? I'm very much aware that the cave had actually helped me but would not solve all my problems. I expected that the cave was only the beginning of a long and vigorous literary career. However, it was not the time for me to worry about that. I had more important things to do. I would have to reunite the "opposing forces" and help Christine find herself. These goals get me closer to the ruins and moments later I'm touching the remains of the symbol of Christianity. I look for the crucifix that was left intact and upon touching it I begin to understand more about my religion and its founder. He had given himself up for us simply for a love that we can't understand. A love so great it was able to perform miracles. That's what I needed: A miracle.

I was about to face unknown forces that fed off of egoism, addictions, weaknesses and human hatred, forces that were able to destroy human life. I look again at the crucifix and it fills me with courage. There was an example of a winner. He was also a dreamer like me and his teachings have conquered the world. He taught us to love and respect others and this was the message that I preached in my day to day. I look around at everything that is near me: I see people, the blue sky, and far away, the horizon. I couldn't disappoint them or myself. With all the strength in my chest, I yell:

— I'm ready!

The earth began to tremble and within seconds I feel snatched from the place where I was. I am led by the hair and the emotion of the moment obscures my vision, everything is dark and empty.

The Experience in the Desert

I have just woken up and I get up to know exactly where I am. I look in the four directions and I can only see sand and the sky. It felt like I was in the middle of the desert. What was I doing here? What kind of joke was this? In an instant, I was at the ruins of the chapel (in Mimoso) and in another I was in this dark, empty place. I begin to walk, looking for something. Who knows maybe I'll find an oasis or someone who can guide me and tell me exactly where I am. The feeling of loneliness increases every minute despite my belief that I am always accompanied by an angel. In these moments I end up reminding myself of how important it is to have friends or someone you can trust. Money, social ostentation, vanities, success and victory are pointless if you don't have someone with whom to share it. I continue to walk and the sweat starts dripping, hunger starts nipping me and thirst does as well. I feel lost as I did in the cave labyrinth. What strategy would I use now? The oasis could be anywhere. I stop for a little bit. I would have to recover my strength and breathe. I had not yet reached my limits but I felt quite tired. The hike up the steep staircase comes to mind, the one in the Sanctuary of Our Lady of Grace, the guardian site, in trusses. I was just a kid and the effort of the climb had cost me a lot. Upon arriving at the top, I got myself into a safe place for fear of falling off of the steep ridge. My mother lit a candle and paid the promise she had made. The shrine was visited by many tourists and it took on the appearance of the Virgin Mary in that place.

The story was as follows: In 1936, the bandit Virgulino Ferreira, the "Lantern", and his gang rode through Pesqueira where they had committed atrocities against the local farmers. Maria da Luz had asked Conceição what she would do if the Lantern showed up there at that moment. The girl had said: "Oh my, I'd have to figure out a way so that this evil-doer wouldn't be able to harm us". That's when, looking at the mountain ridge, they saw an image in the shape of a woman. The apparition repeated in the following days and the news spread throughout the region. The Vatican has admitted that Our Lady of Grace appeared in Pesqueira and in five more locations in different parts of the earth. The apparition at the watch site was the only registered in the American continent.

Upon descending the sanctuary, I felt more relaxed and confident. That's how I would feel upon finding an oasis. I return to my walk and have a question on my mind that will not get out of my head. Where was the challenge? It didn't make sense for me to keep walking without answers. Since I had made the trip to the holy mountain, accomplished the challenges and entered the cave I had had a plan and a purpose. I was now adrift and without direction. I begin to contemplate the skies and I see some birds. A great idea pops into my head and I decide to follow them like I did with the bat in the cave. After thirty minutes into the chase, I see a lake where the birds land and my hope is returned with a greater force. I near the lake and start drinking its water. I drink a little but the bad taste makes me stop. So I sit for a little by the lake to rest my legs and feet which were tired from the trip. A moment later, a hand touches my shoulder and I turn back. The guardian who I met on the mountain was directly in front of me.

— You, here? I wasn't expecting that.

— My son, you look a little tired. Don't you want to go home? Your family misses you very much.

— I can't. I have to fulfill my mission. It was the same lady who sent me to Mimoso to reunite the "opposing forces" and to help Christine.

— Forget your mission. You do not have the strength to defeat your opponent. Remember that even your master Jesus Christ perished on the cross for having disobeyed the Devil.

— You are mistaken. Jesus Christ came out the winner of that dispute and the cross is the symbol of his victory. Wait. You've never spoken that way. Who are you? I am sure that you are not the guardian despite your appearance.

The woman gave a cry of sarcasm and disappeared. So it was just a vision wanting to mess with me. I would have to be very careful with appearances. I remain seated without any ideas as how to leave that extensive and empty place. I only feel my heart throb, my legs twitching and my subconscious saying it's not over. What was missing? I already am tired of this challenge. I look to the horizon and in the distance I see someone approaching. Was it more than just a vision? I would have to be careful. As I got closer I was frightened and couldn't believe it. The person hugs me and I return it in spite of the mistrust.

— Are you really my mother? How did you get here?

— I am. The guardian helped me locate you. After you left, I went to the mountain as I was very worried. So I found the guardian and she guided me.

— Wait. I have to have proof that you are really my mother. What was the name of my favorite cat and which nickname did my nephews give me?

— That is easy. The name of your favorite cat was Pecho and your nickname is Uncle Divinha.

The answer calms me and I embrace her. I really needed someone familiar in that desert.

— What are you doing here?

— I'm here to convince you to give up all of this. You are risking great danger in this desert. Come on, let's go. I shouldn't have let you leave the house.

— I can't. I have to complete a mission. I need to reunite the "opposing forces" and help Christine. In addition, I have to document everything in a book so that I can start my literary career.

— This mission of yours is crazy. You cannot defeat the forces of darkness nor can you publish a book. How many times do I have to say that writing books is not going to bring you any results? You're poor and unknown. Who will buy them? In addition, you have no talent.

— You are completely mistaken. I can reunite the "opposing forces" and make my dream come true. I can't believe that you're my mother even though she didn't encourage me either. I know she has a glimmer of hope that I will really become a writer. I have talent or else I wouldn't have entered the cave to ask the mountain to turn me into the Seer.

Instantly, my mother became a man of light-colored appearance and with eyes of fire. I was a little shocked, but I suspected it wasn't her. The man began to revolve around me.

— Seer, Son of God. Have you ever thought about what all these names mean? Clairvoyance is a gift that helps an individual know the future or have the exact notion of what's going on elsewhere. You do not have these abilities. Actually, what you have is an underdeveloped clairvoyance. It's pretty pretentious of you to claim to be a powerful psychic. As for the fact that you are the Son of God, that is a big joke. Do you not remember the mistakes you committed in a desert exactly like this one? Do you think God forgave you? How then do you have the nerve to call yourself Son of God? To me, you're more of a devil than son of God. That's right. You're the Devil, like me!

— I may not be a powerful psychic, but I get messages from the Creator. He tells me that I will have a bright future. I'm building it every day in my work, in my studies and in the books I write. As for my mistakes, I know them and I have asked forgiveness. Who doesn't make mistakes? I've focused on becoming a new man and I have forgotten all of my past. The messages I receive are that God considers me his son and I firmly believe it. Otherwise he wouldn't have rescued me so many times.

With eyes full of tears, I look at the universe and turn my back to my accuser. I give a strong cry.

— I'm not the Devil! I'm a human being who discovered one day that I have an infinite value to God. He saved me from crisis and showed me the way. Now, I want to stay with him and fulfill myself no matter the obstacles and difficulties that I have to overcome. They will mature me and I will become a better human being. I'll be happy because the universe conspires for that.

The Devil backed away a little and said:

— We will meet again, Aldivan. The war between the "opposing forces" is just beginning. In the end, I will come out the winner.

With that said, he was gone. The instant after, again I'm enraptured. Within seconds I find myself in the previous scenario, again under the ruins of the chapel. I resolve immediately to return to the hotel in order to rest and to recover my strength and spirit. The first challenge had been completed, now there were only two remaining.

The Worshipers of Darkness

The next day, I go back to the same spot where I had been taken to the first experience. Unconsciously, I think that it is the gateway to the challenges. When I look at the ruins, I feel my heart torn apart by the desolation of the place. The true path had been smothered by a wicked and perverse witch. Now, my job was to balance the "opposing forces" and resume the peace lost in that place. Ready, I repeat the password from the day before and again I am transported. I find myself in a strange and dark place where a ritual is being performed. There are about ten people, arranged in circles muttering words in a language I don't know. In the middle, a man is squatting and the others are pouring a liquid with an unbearable odor on his head. A moment later, two horns grow on his head and his countenance becomes terrible looking. He sees me and gets up. He approaches, picks up a sword and throws another one at me. I get nervous because I was not used to dealing with weapons.

He calls me to fight and begins to strike some blows. I try to block them with my sword and I do so, almost by miracle. He continues attacking and I defend myself. I start watching his movements in order to make subsequent reactions. He is quite fast and skillful. Gradually, I begin to fight back and he appears surprised. One of my moves hurts him but he still appears indefatigable. So, I resolve to appeal. I approach him and without him noticing, prepare for a final attack. The sword helps me unbalance him and with clenched fists I hit him with everything I have. He falls to the ground, unconscious. At the same time, I'm transported to the ruins of the chapel. The second challenge was met.

The Experience of Possession

The third day was finally here. Again I go to the chapel ruins. The third experience was marked and I couldn't wait any longer. What was awaiting me? I really don't know but I felt ready for anything. The guardian, the challenges and the cave had contributed significantly to this. I was now the Seer and could no longer be afraid. Confident and calm I repeat the password from the day before. A cold wind hits, my body shakes and incessant voices begin to disturb me. In an instant, my conscience is transported to my mind and upon arriving there, I hear someone knocking on a door. I resolve to answer it. Upon opening the door, a light-colored subject, slim, with honey-colored eyes and a crown of thorns on his head comes in.

— Who are you?

— I am Jesus Christ. Don't you recognize my crown? It was with it that they wounded my head.

— What are you doing here, in my mind?

— I came to take possession of you. If you agree, I will make you the most powerful and the most talented of men.

— How do I know you are who you say you are? I want proof.

— That is easy. You are a young man of twenty-six, quiet, nice and very intelligent. Your dream is to become a writer and that is why you made the trip to a mountain that all claim to be sacred. You met the guardian, the young girl, the ghost, the boy, defeated challenges and entered the most dangerous cave in the world. Dodging traps and advancing scenarios, you won. So it fulfilled your dream and turned you into the Seer. However, the cave was just one step in your spiritual growth. Now, you need me to continue the path.

— So you're really Jesus Christ. However, I don't know if I want someone in my mind. It's hard to get used to a voice guiding me all the time. You can't help me from Heaven? It would be more comfortable for me.

— If I do not stay here, you will become a failure. Decide quickly: Do you want to be a man or do you want to be a God? If you choose the second option I will make you fly, walk on water and perform miracles.

— I don't believe it. Again, I need proof.

I turn my body to a floodplain, where the river passes Mimoso. I wanted to have real proof of what was happening to me. Upon arriving at the river I try to take my first steps on the water. Upon crossing it I am shown proof of his deceit. I was being deceived.

— Monster! You are not Jesus Christ! Get out of my mind now, I command you!

The man was transformed into a creature with horns and a long tail. A strong wind began to blow over him and pushed him right to the entrance door of my mind. He exits and the door is closed. My conscience returns to normal and I feel better. The experience had exhausted my strength and so I resolve to return immediately to the hotel with the third challenge met. Now I only had to convince Christine and to leave for the final battle.

The Prison

Upon arriving at the hotel, I'm surprised by the presence of Delegate Pompeu and his subordinates.

— Well, look who has arrived, just who we were hoping for. Mr. Seer, you sir, are under arrest. (Pompeu)

— How? What is the accusation?

— He is being imprisoned by order of Queen Clemilda and that is enough.

Quickly, the subordinates put handcuffs on me. A mixture of indignation and anger fill my whole being. The Forces of Darkness were using their last resort to prevent the triumph of good. Imprisoned I could not do anything and with this Mimoso would be lost. What would happen to the "opposing forces" and to Christine? In this exact moment I already had lost all hope. They ordered me to walk and that's exactly what I do. On the way to the station, all the injustices I suffered in my life come to mind: A poorly corrected test, an inhumane public attendant, a bad trial and incomprehension from others. In all these situations I felt the same way: downtrodden. I direct my attention to the delegate and I ask him if he does not feel remorse. He says that he doesn't, but he would if he did not fulfill the order as he certainly would lose his job. I understand his point and I have no more questions. Sometime later, we arrive at our destination. They remove my handcuffs and put me in a cell where there are some other prisoners. I spend my first night completely locked up.

Dialog

In little time I find a way to fit in with the other prisoners. They are there for several reasons: One for stealing chickens, others for refusing to pay taxes and some because they did not vote for the candidate nominated by the major. Among them is Claudio. I begin to chat with him.

— Have you been here long?

— Yes, a long time. I've been here ever since the major discovered that I was dating his daughter. And you, why are you in jail?

— Well, I had a disagreement with a lady called Clemilda. She has committed tyranny locking me in here like this. But tell me about yourself, you love this girl so much to the point that you risked facing the major?

— Yes, I love her. Ever since I met Christine, I am a new man. I have come to appreciate the really important things. I also gave up my bad habits and wild ways. Without her, I don't know what will become of my life.

— I understand. The moment that I met her, I thought she was really special. It's a shame she had to go through such a tragedy.

— I heard about the tragedy here, in prison. However, I refuse to believe that the woman that I love is a murderer. Her temperament does not correspond with that fact.

— She was just another victim of the witch Clemilda. This creature unbalanced the "opposing forces" and it threatens the entire universe. So it was left to fate to have to send me to the sacred mountain where I met the guardian, the young girl, the ghost, and the boy. I completed the challenges and with that conquered the right to enter the cave of despair, the cave that grants your deepest dreams. Dodging traps and advancing scenarios I managed to reach the end. Then the cave transformed me into the Seer and I made a trip in time following a scream I heard. This scream was from Christine. Upon arriving at the current day I stood up to Clemilda and she gave me three challenges which I completed. Now the only thing that remains to do is to convince your beloved in order to have a final battle. However, I am now in prison and that prevents me from taking any action.

— What a story! I already had heard of the cave and its wonderful powers but never imagined that someone could overcome it. You were the first that I heard speak of it. Look, if you need my help, I'm available.

— Thank You. Is there any way to escape from here?

— I am sorry, but there is not. These gates are very strong and the building's exits are all monitored.

Claudio's reply disheartened me. What would become of the "opposing forces," Christine and Mimoso? Every passing moment things were getting worse with me in prison. Now, the only thing to do was to pray and wait for a miracle.

Renato's Visit

I have just woke up and the feeling I felt, like everything was wrong, does not make me feel good at all. This place was not suitable for me because I was affected by the high negative charge. The "opposing forces" shouted inside me and were more active than ever. A little later, one of the guards comes and opens the cell for us to go out into the sun. I enter the queue that is formed. We walk around a bit and in little time we are returned to the cell. Upon returning, I am informed that someone awaits me in the visiting area. A guard accompanies me and I go to meet this person. Upon entering the visiting room, I'm surprised.

— You? What are you doing here, boy?

— I came to help you. The time has now come for me to prove that I am useful and that the guardian was right to send me to accompany you.

— Help me? How?

— Don't worry. I already have everything planned. When everything happens don't think twice, run.

— What are you intending to do? Isn't it dangerous?

— I cannot say anything. Just do what I say.

— Thank you, but don't risk so much just for me. You are only a child.

— I am a child but I do know how to distinguish a human heart. I feel that you are a very special person.

Renato's words touch me and I embrace him. He's been with me virtually the whole time since the trip began and this has created affection between us. I already felt like his father but at that moment he was the one consoling and encouraging me. After the embrace, he says goodbye and I go back to the cell, accompanied by a guard. I find Claudio and we start a new conversation. Approximately thirty minutes after Renato's departure, I smell an odd smell, smoke covers the enclosure and all begin to panic, including myself. The delegate is called and orders all cells to be opened. In the confusion, I remember Renato's advice and I direct myself out of the police station without anyone seeing me as the smoke is so dense. On the way out, I find Renato and we escape together. We go back to the hotel and there Carmen puts us in a special room. It had an underground entrance and there we were housed. I would be safe until the final battle.

The Third Encounter with Christine

Christine finally decided and was willing to meet with me again. She heard that I had been arrested and this fact helped her to decide. She also was weary of the injustices committed by her father and by the evil sorceress Clemilda. In a certain way, she already controlled her "opposing forces" and this had been paramount in her decision. So she decided to find Carmen, the owner of the hotel. She was sure that Carmen knew something of my whereabouts. She claps her hands at the entrance of the hotel and was immediately attended to.

— The Descent from the Mountain

— Are you Ms. Carmen? I need to speak with you ma'am.

— Yes. Come in.

Christine answered the invitation and went in. Carmen went to fetch tea and biscuits. She comes back with a captivating smile.

— What can I do for you, dear? (Carmen)

— I'm looking for Aldivan, the Seer. He was in jail but today I heard that he escaped from prison. Do you have any idea where he is? It is important.

— I have no idea. Since he was arrested I stopped having contact with him.

— It's not possible. I need both him and Mimoso so much. So then everything will just remain as always? Just how long will we take Clemilda's dictatorship?

Tears pour down Christine's face and she goes into despair. Her reaction moves Carmen and she goes to comfort her.

— If this meeting with him is so important then I think I can find a way.

Carmen moves away from the living room for a moment and calls me into a room. Upon learning about the presence of Christine I become happy and resolve immediately to go see her. I turn back towards the living room while Renato remains in the room and Carmen goes to the kitchen to get dinner ready. When she sees me, Christine gets up and runs to hug me. I reciprocate the affection. We sat side by side in the room.

— So, have you decided?

— I have thought a lot about what you said and I want to say that I believe it. In the convent, they taught me to recognize when a person is sincere.

— In addition to believing, are you are willing to change your life?

— Yes and I want to forget everything that happened. You were right about the fact that I am not guilty of the tragedy. It was a curse that that witch launched on me when she touched my head. I still have hopes that she is defeated and that the wish I made to the mountain is granted.

— So I did it. You found yourself. You no longer seem to be the sad, dismayed young girl. I am happy for you. Now I can have the right to a final battle. The encounter of the "opposing forces" is approaching.

— Battle? What are you talking about?

— It is the deal that I made with Clemilda. If I fulfilled three challenges and convinced you to find your destiny, I would have the right to this battle. It is the only chance to gather the "opposing forces" and balance them once again.

— I understand. Can I help? My mutant powers would be of great help in battle.

— I don't know. It's very dangerous. If you get hurt, Christine, I wouldn't be able to forgive myself.

I think for a few moments about her proposal. I wonder if she would really be necessary on the battlefield. I didn't know what kind of war this would be.

— All right, you can. However, you must stay behind me. I will protect you from the Forces of Darkness. Meanwhile, you cover the rear with your mutant powers.

— Thank you. When will this happen?

— Tomorrow. Meet me at the chapel ruins at 7:00 AM.

I take my leave and ask her to keep my location a secret. She agrees and leaves. A certain repentance eats at me for having accepted a battle but it is too late. The next day would be final in regards to the fate of Mimoso and I would participate in a battle that would completely change my life and certainly the universe too.

The Angel's Invocation

Christine and I arrived on time at the rendezvous point. She asks me why this particular site and I answer that this was the gateway to my experiences. I explain to her the details about the "opposing forces" and the current imbalance. After that, I ask for silence and start to invoke the Angel because it would be of great help in battle.

— The war between the "opposing forces" approaches. In this fight, material and immaterial beings will face each other. Our group consists of only two people: I, the Seer, and Christine, who is a mutant. We need a higher power to give us an intangible security so we ask of Our Father, to send his Angel to accompany and protect us in this perilous fight. Mimoso's fate hangs in the balance and the strength of goodness has to be complete.

I repeat the prayer three times and on the last I feel my heart trembling with irregular beats and my sixth sense becomes fully sharpened. A moment later, my doors are open and I have permission to unlock the mysteries of the other world. I see, in a large room of a royal palace, a door opened and from it leave seven angels that together represent God himself. One of them carries a goblet in his hand whose contents is my insistent prayer. The seven angels approach the throne of the Almighty God. The one that has the chalice spills it over the fire on the right side of the Father. Thunder roars and altered voices are heard. The door between the two worlds is opened and the angel with the chalice goes through it. The door is sealed and locked until its return. At that moment, my doors are closed and I return to normal. Upon regaining consciousness, I see Christine kneeling and beside me a blazing Angel with long and bright wings, lighting the entire place. On its face is written King of Kings and Lord of Lords. Its feet and legs seem to be on fire and its slender body overcomes any sculpture. I stand by for a few moments admiring its beauty. It decides to contact me through the forces of thought. It asks me to keep calm and raise Christine to her feet because she had no reason to worship him. I obey the Angel and ask it what's going to happen. It tells me that it doesn't know, that the meeting between the "opposing forces" is unpredictable. It assures me that we will be safe with it. With renewed forces and celestial protection, I resolve to try the same password of my previous experience. With all the strength in my chest, I yell:

— We are ready!

The ground shakes, the sky darkens, the stars are shattered and the entire universe feels the emotion of the moment. The final battle would start and the future of both worlds was at stake.

The Final Battle

The scenario is still changing. The floor disappears and the angel has to give us powers so that we can also fly. On the horizon a dividing line appears as a type of force field which prevents us from passing. Then comes the moment in which everything begins. An immense darkness approaches along with a vampire and some hooded men. On the other side is Clemilda, commanding everything with her Machiavellian super-powers. The fight finally begins. The angel and the demon, Christine and the vampire, and I and the hooded men. The fight between intangible beings is simply unimaginable. The two move with incredible speed and their blows are extremely powerful. With every impact, the two worlds appear to tremble. The clash between Christine and the vampire is also equally balanced. She uses her rays of fire to protect herself from his assaults. I am also encountering difficulty. The hooded men are skilled fighters. I must use all of my clairvoyant powers to confront them. The war between the "opposing forces" was only just beginning and the difficulties were numerous.

The fight continues and the clash gradually begins to change. Some hooded men drop in exhaustion and I feel freer. The fight between the angel and the demon and Christine and the vampire remained equal but from my point of view good was winning out. In just a few moments, I succeed in overthrowing my recent opponents. Then I rest a little and observe the other's fights. I am hoping for victories for all of them. Clemilda perceives her imminent defeat and with her powers invokes the undead. They leave the tomb of an ancient indigenous cemetery and are all people who in one way or another let themselves divert from their true paths. They are my new opponents in battle. Among them, I recognize indigenous Kualopu, a sorcerer that almost caused the extinction of the Xukuru Nation. He is my most feared adversary because, like Clemilda, he dominates the dark forces. Before starting the fight, I'm beginning to remember the teachings of the guardian, the challenges and the cave. All these steps have served as amazing spiritual growth for me. Now, I would have to use this in my favor in battle. The fight begins and the living dead try to enclose me with the objective of attacking me all at once. I get rid of this siege quickly and attack. With the strength of my attack, some of them rip apart. Kualopu begins to repeat a silent prayer and at the very same moment, a luminous circle secures me and leaves me immobile. The other undead leverage to attack me. The memory of the cave comes forth when I had to confront a whole scenario of mirrors. Three reflections came to life and represented a fifteen year old young man who had lost his father, a child and an old man. I went up against all of these aspects and found that none of them in the present was a twenty-six year old young man, a writer, licensed in mathematics. The circle that held me represented all the weaknesses, that when entering the cave, I managed to control. Thinking about this I focused my powers and with an impulse, the circle is broken. I then could retaliate and destroyed a great number of the undead. Kualopu declined to recognize my strength and with a final blow I was able to overcome him. Upon seeing this, Clemilda panicked and began to articulate her latest strategy.

While Clemilda was preparing, I observed that the other forces of good were already at an advantage against the opposite force. This made me happy and relaxed. I also take the time to relax and catch my breath. Finally Clemilda decides. She leaves to join the fight directly against me. Using dark forces, she arms herself with a sword and shield. The angel sees my situation and with its powers gives me the same weapons. The showdown begins and I am amazed with the agility of my rival. She was no amateur. I remain on the defensive for a time to observe her in all respects. My attitude makes me lose my balance and the sorceress was able to hit me in the face. I reorganize my plans and try to counter-attack. My answer gets results and I get back in the fight. With another lunge, I disarm her and she is left with no defense. Then in order to balance the situation further I also get rid of my armor.

I grab her and we measure our forces. She invokes the Devil and I, Jesus Christ and his cross. At that same moment, she falls defeated. The demon and the vampire disappear; the sun and the ground appear. The angel shines more than ever and I can hear from Heaven a noise of great festivity. I had managed to gather the "opposing forces" and help Christine. In an instant, the angel says goodbye and also disappears. My trip in time had been a success and I would repeat it whenever it was necessary to do so.

The Collapse of the Existing Structures

With the fall of Clemilda, the black clouds dissipated, her henchmen fled and Christine was healed. With this, Mimoso returned to normal and Christianity resumed its place. To celebrate, Christine organized a celebration in the building of the Residents' Association. I was the main guest. The party was full of reporters who kept asking questions.

— Is it true, Mr. Seer, that you saved Mimoso from the claws of an evil sorceress? How did this happen?

— Well, I was only an instrument of destiny as well as my fighting companion here, Christine. The "opposing forces" were imbalanced and my mission was to reunite them again.

— What are you going to do now, Sir?

— Well, I don't know. I think that I must wait for a new adventure.

— Are you married, Sir? What is your profession?

— No. I am prioritizing my studies. About my profession, I am an administrative assistant. In addition, I am licensed in mathematics and am a writer.

The questions continue but I pull away from the reporters. I am going to talk with Christine and see how she is. She says that she forgot the tragedy but she's still concerned about Claudio. He was arrested some time ago and she's had no news. She reaffirms her love and says that he is unforgettable. I console her and try to cheer her up. During the party, I stay by her side to give her strength. When it ends, I bid her farewell and I return to the hotel.

Conversation with the Major

Before leaving Mimoso, I decided to make one last effort for Christine. A great love such as hers and Claudio's could not go without one last chance. So I went to the residence of the feared major for a final conversation with him. Upon entering the garden of the house, I announced myself and shortly after was in front of him.

— Mr. Major, I came to speak to you about your beautiful daughter Christine. I was just with her and realized she is suffering. Why don't you give a chance to the tax collector, Claudio? Look, don't you see how he is the most appropriate man for her?

— Do not involve yourself in family matters. I did not raise my daughter to have a tax collector as my son-in-law.

— I'm involving myself because I am her friend and her happiness matters to me. Your Majesty rejects Claudio because he is poor and simple. Have you forgotten your poor childhood in Maceió? Your Majesty has also been simple. What matters in a human being are his qualities, his talent and charisma. Our social status does not define us. We are what our deeds say of us.

My answer shakes the major some and insistent tears flow from his eyes. He wipes them away in shame.

— How do you know this? I never told anyone about this dark part of my life.

— You wouldn't understand even if I explained it. The problem is that you are being unfair with Christine and depriving her of true love. Do you see the tragedy that you provoked with your arranged marriage? That system does not work.

The major was thoughtful for a few moments and soon after replied.

— Fine. I'll allow the two to date and then to marry but I do not want to see them here close by. My daughter continues to be a disappointment in my life.

— And as for Claudio? Will you release him?

— Yes, today.

— Major, one more thing. I quit my job as your journalist. I can't stand lying to these people anymore about you.

The major writhed in anger but I was already headed out. Upon leaving, I enjoy a clear conscience because I had fulfilled my role. Now, all that was left to destiny was to join the two hearts that really loved one another.

Farewell

Finally, the moment arrived for Claudio to be set free. Outside the police precinct, he waited for his friends and the impassioned Christine. All were eager and nervous for the occasion. Inside the station, Claudio signs the last papers to be released.

— I am finished, Delegate Pompeu. Can I go already? It was a time of much suffering and anguish inside here. I remember well the day that they locked me in here and it was the worst day of my life. (Claudio)

— You can go now. See if you can't keep away from flirting with girls you shouldn't be, eh?

— My arrest was tyrannical and you know it, sir. Is it a crime to love? I do not control my heart.

— Well, you've been warned. Soldier Peixoto accompanies the subject up to the exit.

Claudio withdraws and the soldier obeys the orders of the delegate. On the way out, Claudio looked slightly backwards as if saying goodbye to the moments he had spent in prison. After, he looked up to the sky as if to take into account the entire universe. He felt free and happy because he would be recommencing his life. Moments later, he was embracing his friends and Christine waited her turn. The two embraced and they kissed at length.

— My love! You are free! Now we can be happy because my father has allowed our relationship. The mountain is really sacred because it answered our request. (Christine)

— Is this true? I don't believe it! Does that mean we can be together and have our children? Blessed mountain. I did not expect this miracle.

The two continued to commemorate and in the meantime I approach. We were reaching the time of my departure.

— How wonderful to see you together and happy. I think I can return, rest-assured, back to my real time.

— Do you really have to go? What a pity! Look how we've learned to admire your efforts and determination. I will never forget what you have done for me and for Claudio, thank you!

— I will miss you too. In prison, where we were held together, I got to know you a little and I think you deserve a chance in life and in the universe. Good luck! (Claudio)

— Before I go, I want to ask one last thing, Christine. Can I publish a book with your story?

— Yes, with one condition. I want to title it.

— All right. What is it?

— It will be called "Opposing Forces."

I approve of Christine's indication and give them one last embrace. They all were a part of my story. With tears in my eyes, I back away and direct myself to the hotel. I would pack my suitcases and leave. Along the way, I remember all the times I had in that rustic place. Everything that I had gone through had contributed to my spiritual and moral formation. Now, I was prepared for new adventures and perspectives. With slow steps, I approach the hotel. I say farewell for the last time to everything that is around me and I conclude that I will not forget them completely. They will be forever etched in my mind as memories from my first trip in time, a trip which changed the history of small village called Mimoso. Thinking about it, I feel happy and fulfilled. A few moments later, I arrive at the hotel and I go to my room. Renato is sleeping and I wake him. We pack our suitcases and go to the kitchen in order to say goodbye to Carmen.

— Ms. Carmen, we are leaving. I wanted to say that your aid was very important for me to find out the details of the tragedy. In addition, I would like to thank you for your hospitality and patience.

— It is I who would like to thank you for all that you've done for Mimoso. We lived under a dictatorship and you have freed us. I hope all of your dreams come true.

— Thank You. Renato, say good-bye to Ms. Carmen.

— I want to say that you have been like a mother to me during all this time. I loved the food and your advice.

The three of us embraced and the emotion of the moment made me shed some tears. What we had lived during these thirty days was coming to an end. She would be forever special in my life. When the embrace ended, we walked to the door and waved a final goodbye. Upon leaving, we would head for the same point where we completed the trip back in time.

The Return

From the outside of the hotel, I take one last look at that which had been my home during these thirty days. There I had had my first vision that showed me a whole story. It was the realization of the dreams of the Seer, an omniscient being, through his visions. With the facts, I was able to enter the timetable of events and act so that the injustices were undone. This left me with a clear, happy conscience because I had fulfilled the mission that the guardian had entrusted to me. I had managed to reunite the "opposing forces" and help Christine to find true happiness. Consequently, Mimoso returned to Christianity and many of its faithful could worship, praise and magnify the Creator. I wish I could have had a little more time to enjoy all this work. Well, I will be observing in spirit. With a glance, I look at Renato and realize how he was important in my mission. Without him, my contact with Christine would not have been adequately done nor would I have escaped from prison. It had really been worthwhile to take him on this journey.

We continue to walk and quickly approach the foot of the Ororubá Mountain, the mountain that all considered sacred. It was there that I met the guardian, the ghost, the young woman and the child, I completed challenges and I entered into the most dangerous cave in the world. Inside the cave, dodging traps and advancing scenarios I managed to have it carry out my dream and it changed me into the Seer. All this had been extremely important so I could make the trip in time and alter the line of events. Now I was there, at the foot of the mountain, fulfilled and already thinking about the next adventure. I was so concentrated on this that little did I realize a small hand was pulling me. I turned to see what was going on. It was Renato.

— What will become of me now, Mr. Seer?

— Well, I shall return you to the guardian who cares for you, right?

— Promise that you will take me on your next trip. I loved staying thirty days in the village of Mimoso. For the first time, I felt useful and important.

— I don't know. Only if it is strictly necessary. We will see.

My answer seems not to have made Renato exactly happy but I don't mind. I could not guarantee anything about the future despite being psychic. In addition, I could not predict what would happen with the book that I would publish. On it my new adventures depended. I forget a bit about the issue of the book and I concentrate in the surrounding nature: The gray clouds, the pure air, the exuberant vegetation and the hot sun. The seven days that I had spent at the top of the mountain had taught me to respect it fully. When we do not do this, it responds negatively. The examples are not few: Natural disasters, global warming and the scarcity of natural resources. The end is near if we remain in this state of irrationality.

Time passes and we climb the mountain completely. We return to the point where we made the trip in time and I start to concentrate. I create a circle of light around us and we begin to slow down. It was necessary to do the opposite of what was done previously to move forward in time. A cold wind hits, my heart accelerates, the gravitational forces lose power and with this we can begin to make the return journey. The ring of light expands and the years go passing by: 1910, 1920, 1930, 1940, 1950, 1960, ... 2010. When we got exactly at that point, the circle became undone and we fall to the floor. Upon getting up, I see the guardian and this makes me happier.

— So then, I see you have come back already. You managed to reunite the "opposing forces" and help the girl, Child of God?

— Yes. The trip was a success and I managed to reorder the meaning of things. The cave was very important in order for me to be successful.

— The cave will be just one step on your path. It should serve as support for growth and learning. The Seer still has many challenges to face. Be wise and prudent in your decisions.

— Well, I am returning Renato to you. You were right in sending him with me. He was important. In addition, I would like to thank you for all the attention and dedication that you gave me. Without your teachings, I would not have beat the cave nor become the Seer.

— Do not thank me yet. You must return to this sacred place whenever necessary. Then I will appear and will show you the path. Before anything, remember: Love and faith are two powerful forces that when correctly used produce miracles. When in doubt or during your soul's darkest night, cling to your God and to these two forces. They will free you.

Having said that, the guardian disappeared along with Renato. I stood a few moments thinking about what the guardian said. My soul's darkest night? I think I should learn more about that. I grabbed my suitcases and I started down the mountain. I would catch the first car to go back home.

At Home

I have just returned from my voyage and my relatives receive me with a party. My mother seems worried as she is relentless in asking me questions. I answer some and she becomes calmer. I go to my room to put away my suitcases. Again I look at the works that I've read in recent years and I feel even happier because soon mine is to be amongst them. I am now part of literature and feel very proud of it. My attention deviates and I note that my bed is full of math books. I feel a little guilty for having abandoned them for a little over a month. I start leafing through them, doing a few calculations. Finally, I'm back to doing mathematics, the other passion of my life.

Epilogue

After abandoning Mimoso, many things happened. Christine and Claudio married and became parents to seven beautiful children. The small chapel of St. Sebastian was rebuilt and the governor completed his promise to the major and supported him for Mayor of Pesqueira. He was elected and continued his history of domination and authoritarianism. In the recent past, the highway BR-232 was built and that brought about the transfer of services and business to Arcoverde (during the time the book was written it was Rio Branco Village). Then came the gradual disengagement of the railroad and Mimoso became a ghost town.

Currently, Mimoso has three-thousand inhabitants and the economy of the district is linked to neighboring cities, Pesqueira and Arcoverde. Basically, it rotates around the production and cattle-breeding salaries received by its retired people. One of the highlights of Mimoso is the foundation Possidônio Tenório de Brito, which through the retired judge Aluiz Tenório de Brito, offers opportunities for education and culture. He installed a valuable library, started up an Informational Education course and also started a video library. I'm one of the young people who benefited from this initiative and today I'm a writer, author of "Opposing Forces."

The End.